"What you need is a man who appreciates you for what you are."

"And I suppose you think you're that man?"

"I don't think it; I know it."

His confidence in himself was too much, especially when hers was so low. She didn't need him in her life now. Didn't want him... Ah, there was the real kicker. She'd never stopped wanting him.

"You conceited bastard." she said, planting her fists on her hips and walking to within a foot of him. "Who do you think you are, coming back here and feeding me this line of bull after leaving me alone for six years?"

"Isn't that what you wanted me to do—leave you alone?"

He had her there. "You bet it was!" she snapped. "It's still what I want. You say you want to try again, but you'd better face facts, Lattimer. I'm just not the marrying kind—and I've got the divorce papers to prove it."

Dear Reader,

Spellbinders! That's what we're striving for. The editors at Silhouette are determined to capture your imagination and win your heart with every single book we publish. Each month, six Special Editions are chosen with *you* in mind.

Our authors are our inspiration. Writers such as Nora Roberts, Tracy Sinclair, Kathleen Eagle, Carole Halston and Linda Howard—to name but a few—are masters at creating endearing characters and heartrending love stories. Their characters are everyday people—just like you and me—whose lives have been touched by love, whose dreams and desires suddenly come true!

So find a cozy, quiet place to read, and create your own special moment with a Silhouette Special Edition.

Sincerely,

The Editors
SILHOUETTE BOOKS

BAY MATTHEWS
Some Warm Hunger

Silhouette Special Edition

Published by Silhouette Books New York

America's Publisher of Contemporary Romance

For my very own equine dentists,
Todd and Bret—my sons and sometime heroes.
Special thanks to my editor, Phyliss Lefkowitz,
for all her helpful suggestions and
for making me step back and take another look.

SILHOUETTE BOOKS
300 East 42nd St., New York, N.Y. 10017

Copyright © 1987 by Penny Richards

ISBN: 0-373-09391-8

First Silhouette Books printing July 1987

America's Publisher of Contemporary Romance

Printed in the U.S.A.

Books by Bay Matthews

Silhouette Special Edition

Bittersweet Sacrifice #298
Roses and Regrets #347
Some Warm Hunger #391

BAY MATTHEWS

of Haughton, Louisiana, describes herself as a dreamer and an incurable romantic. Married at an early age to her high school sweetheart, she claims she grew up with her three children. Now that only the youngest is at home, writing romances adds a new dimension to the already exciting life she leads on her husband's thoroughbred farm.

Prologue

The sound of flesh meeting flesh when Bodie Lattimer's fist crashed into a slack-jawed face could be heard even over the low roar of the tavern's conversation and the sad statement—via the jukebox—that cowboys didn't get lucky all the time. Which, Bodie thought fleetingly, swearing and shaking the abused hand against the numbing pain shooting up his arm, was an understatement.

Catching his opponent off guard, the big farmer type smashed his fist into Bodie's mouth, snapping his head backward and splitting his lip. Bodie gave a low grunt of pain, but didn't fall. He wasn't exactly a featherweight himself. Balling his hands into fists, he brought his right forward, putting the full force of his two hundred and eight pounds behind the swing that landed with a solid thud in his antagonist's beer belly.

The man doubled over with a low retching sound, and Bodie reached out to haul him upright again.

Immediately, a half-dozen pairs of hands were separating the two brawlers and Bodie was ushered none-to-gently to the exit of the smoky, crowded establishment.

"It wasn't my fault!" he growled, struggling without success against the restraining hands and protesting his innocence all the way to the door. As usual, he refused to back down from his claim that it wasn't his fault. But then, it never was. And, as usual, his protestations fell on deaf ears. The men shoved him out the door into an Illinois May night, and the grill of a dusty pickup caught his ribs in a bruising embrace.

The proprietor tossed Bodie's straw Western hat toward him and it sailed to the ground near his feet. "Look, Mister, why don't you just get in that fancy rig of yours and head outta here?" he suggested.

Bodie blotted the corner of his mouth with the heel of his hand and regarded the blood with a frown. Maybe discretion really was the better part of valor, he thought, reaching for his hat and putting it on before pulling himself to his feet with the aid of the pickup's grill.

"Good idea." He managed a sardonic smile out of the uninjured side of his mouth and rammed a work-roughened hand into the pocket of his Wranglers, which were softened and faded from numerous washings, and molded themselves perfectly to his long legs and flat, masculine buttocks.

Drawing out a set of keys, he saluted smartly in the general direction of the sextet guarding the doorway and ambled toward the metallic-blue Bronco spotlighted by the neon glow of a sign that told the world that this was Bud's Place. He unlocked the door and slid inside, revving the engine to life and reversing out of the parking lot with a spray of gravel. He pulled onto the highway with a sigh of relief and without a backward glance. It wasn't a night he wanted to remember.

It was after midnight when he pulled into a Holiday Inn just south of St. Louis. He was, as his Uncle Jake used to say, "dead-dog tired," and the kingsize bed held an unmistakable lure. Ignoring his exhaustion, he stripped the plaid shirt from his broad torso. As much as the bed drew him, right now he wanted nothing more than to wash the Illinois dust from his pores and the smell of Bud's Place from his mind. He was heartsick of places like that. Heartsick and soul weary of motels and airplanes and the gray ribbon of highway stretching from ocean to ocean.

He put the toe of one boot against the heel of the other and inched off his worn work boots, whose cracked leather held the unmistakable odor of horse manure. His socks followed. His Wranglers and white Fruit of the Looms were left in a pile on the floor before he cast a last, longing look toward the bed and headed for the bathroom.

The water was hot and held the promise of at least satisfying half his wants as the soap and water washed away the dirty feeling left after a day's travel. Forgetting the incident was another matter. His mind was running full tilt as he lathered his head with the small bar of soap the motel provided. The beer he'd consumed two hours earlier was wearing off quickly, leaving his mind wide open to memories of the bar-room brawl. He sighed. Trouble seemed to be his constant companion lately.

All he'd done was tell the woman to leave him alone. He sighed again. Maybe he could have done it with a little more tact, he admitted grudgingly. She must have complained about the rudeness of his rejection to some of her friends.

Pressing his palms against the tiled walls, Bodie ducked his soapy head beneath the sharp, needlelike spray. He was genuinely sorry it had ended the way it had, but even though he knew he'd been too long without that pleasant release of body and mind, the thought of a meaningless night with a meaningless woman just didn't turn him on.

Turning off the water and yanking back the shower curtain, he toweled his hair dry then rubbed the towel's white softness over the abundant mat of hair that sprawled across his broad chest and the flatness of his belly. He finished drying his long, muscular legs, then used the towel to wipe the steam from the mirror.

With the damp terry cloth still resting against the shiny glass surface, he stared at the naked man reflected back at him. Thirty-nine. Sometimes he felt sixty. His six-foot, four-inch body was still without an ounce of extra fat, probably because he usually only ate one meal a day. The dark hair on his head, though bearing a patch of gray just behind both ears, was still thick and healthy-looking with no sign of a receding hairline.

There were grooves that time and life had carved into his cheeks, and what some called crow's-feet radiating from his deceptively lazy, dark-green eyes. But those hadn't come with age; they'd always been there from being outside so much, squinting in the sun, and from laughter back in the days when there had been something to laugh about—someone to laugh with. The thought of laughter drew his attention to his mouth, with its bruised and swollen bottom lip. He gave a disgusted grunt, tilting his head sideways and probing the area with a tentative finger. Brawling at his age was ridiculous!

Thirty-nine was high time to mend his ways, find a wife and raise that passel of kids he'd always wanted. The trouble was, it was hard for him to find a good woman, traveling around as he did from racetrack to racetrack, plying his trade as an equine dentist and working for the top trainers who thought nothing of providing the plane tickets to get him where they needed him.

The wry twist of his mouth resembled a smile, then turned into a grimace as his battered lip protested. Ah, yes. The price of success. And no doubt about it, he was a success . . . for whatever that was worth.

He dropped the towel, turned off the bathroom light and went back into the bedroom. A quick flick of his wrist peeled back the covers, and he slid between the sheets, the crisp freshness cool next to his water-warmed body.

Clasping his hands behind his damp head and lowering his head to the pillow, he turned his mind to the upcoming visit he had planned with his family before he would head out to California. It would be good to go home again. Good to see his dad and brothers, good to taste his mother's strawberry pies. Good . . .

Soon the heat from the wall unit combined with his twelve-hours-on-the-road weariness, and Bodie Lattimer succumbed to the welcome arms of sleep...

"Jessie!"

It was almost two hours later when he jerked straight up in bed, the name spilling from his lips in longing and torment, rising from the hidden depths of his heart where he'd buried it years before. The clean, sunshine smell he always associated with her lingered in his nostrils, and the soft darkness of her coffee-colored eyes was still vivid in his sleep-fogged mind. His startled gaze traveled the room, finding it a clone of every motel room in America. He knew where he was then. He was south of St. Louis—not back in Louisiana with Jessie in his arms...in his heart. He bent his legs at the knees and rested his brawny forearms on the twin peaks, breathing heavily and waiting for the rapid beating of his heart to calm.

Jessie Harper. Why was it she always came to him at night, when his defenses were low or nonexistent? Memories of her still stole through his mind and possessed his dreams regardless of how many women there had been these past six years...and in spite of how much beer he drank on those rare occasions when images of her threatened his very sanity.

Images of Jessie saddling a horse in the paddock, her blond mane of hair coiled up in a loose, queenly knot, her face wearing that look of intensity that was so much a part of her as she cinched the girth and smoothed the saddle towel just so. Jessie, the picture of poise and control.

Except in bed.

Bodie swung his feet to the floor and reached for his cigarettes. His lighter flared briefly in the room's darkness, then was replaced with the glowing tip of the cigarette as he dragged deeply on the acrid smoke. He rose from the bed, picked up an ashtray and paced the length of the room with a restlessness that was more and more a part of him.

Jessie in bed. There was nothing calm and poised about her then, a fact that was proven by his body's immediate physical reaction. Another half smile quirked his mouth at the memory. When they had made love it was with a warm hunger that fed off itself until they were both sleepy and sated. He swore and stubbed out the half-smoked cigarette.

"Leave me alone, Jessie!" The words were grated with savage intensity into the darkness. But the plea was useless. She was there. As much a part of the room and the night as the bed that now looked cold and strange without her in it.

He shivered at the old memories and began to pull on his clothes. Dressed in clean jeans and a shirt, he went to the window and drew back the drapes. The spring night was clear, cloudless. The diamond brightness of billions of stars glittered against the velvet backdrop of the night, precious gems scattered across the endless heavens by an unseen hand.

Bodie.... Bodie....

His name sounded in his ears, Jessie's voice calling him back through time, through space, through six endlessly long, lonely years. *Forget her, Lattimer. Give it up. Let her go.*

Dear God, he'd tried. He'd truly tried.

Dropping into the chair by the window, he covered his face with his hands and rested his elbows on his knees, his mind reliving his leaving six years earlier and all the other nights he'd fallen asleep with her name on his lips and tears of regret in his eyes.

Time passed; he was unaware of it. He sat, his feet propped on the windowsill, smoking and thinking until morning began to leech the ebony of the sky to gray, extinguishing the silver shine of the stars one by one. Then the sun began its majestic ascent, turning the sky from gray to salmon, then to gold. Bodie watched it rise, the sight triggering another memory: Jessie waking up after they'd spent the night loving one another. Her lashes would lift slowly, her eyes, warm and brown, would open, focus sleepily on him, then her lips would begin to curve slowly upward and the sunshine of her smile would envelope him, its warmth, like that of the rising sun, spreading throughout him, making him feel whole...more a man...

With a sound that was a cross between a growl of denial and a groan of acquiescence, Bodie ground out the last cigarette, dropped the front legs of the chair to the floor and stood up. He pulled on his socks, eagerness in the steady purpose of his actions. He was going back. And this time he meant to have her. The few times he had allowed their lives to touch he'd kept her firmly at arm's length, kept his emotions hidden beneath the bantering manner he adopted to hide his bleeding heart—a heart that all the Band-Aids in the world couldn't fix.

The sun, still climbing, forced itself through the window, sweeping the last remnants of night into the shadowed corners of the room, sweeping away the doubts and fears arising from his new decision. He stretched mightily to loosen his cramped muscles before he pulled on his boots and let himself out of the room.

The morning air was cool, but springtime was apparent from the sound of the robins chirping in a nearby bush. Bodie, unlocking the Bronco's door and sliding behind the wheel, didn't notice. His mind was on a tall woman with a mass of streaky, dishwater blond hair who could train a horse or tame a man with nothing but soft words and the touch of her capable hands. In a matter of minutes he was headed south, down I-55, ultimately for Louisiana and Jessica Lorene Harper.

Chapter One

Jessie Harper swiped at a strand of loose hair that had been tugged free of her jaunty ponytail by the breeze that was ushering in the new dawn. Frothy cotton-candy clouds dotted the early-morning, abalone-tinted sky. Yet, despite the desultory stirring of the air, the humidity was high and the early May day promised to be a scorcher. Louisiana Downs, the thoroughbred racetrack just outside Bossier City, was alive with the sounds of thundering hooves as horses jogged, galloped or breezed around the oval. Whoops of encouragement were yelled into equine ears, and taunts and obscenities were flung from one rider to another as they sped by.

Jessie leaned against the rail near the clocker's stand, a Styrofoam cup of coffee in one hand, a stopwatch in the other, her brown eyes intent on the horses racing down the stretch. They flew by, slinging clods of dirt out behind them, the sounds of their labored breathing audible to her and the other observing trainers who stood watching nearby. Her thumb depressed the stem of the stopwatch, and a slow smile of satisfaction curved her lips. Her filly, who had been several months coming back after a hairline fracture of the cannon bone, had worked three-eights in thirty-six seconds—not bad, considering how hard it was to get a horse fit after being off so long.

She dropped the watch into the breast pocket of her shirt and sipped at her coffee while she waited for the horse to come back to the gap that led from the track to the stable area.

"There you are!"

The easily recognizable voice halted the coffee cup's ascent to her lips. Dan. The man who, six years ago, had been her husband for just over three months—long enough to father her daughter, Cissy. Jessie straightened and turned, schooling her features into an impassivity she was far from feeling. She leaned against the rail with deceiving nonchalance and watched his approach with as much objectivity as she could muster.

Tall and rangy, Dan Givens was very attractive with his classic features and his blond hair that was always perfectly groomed. Today he was dressed in tasteful light-gray slacks, a short-sleeved dress shirt and tasseled charcoal loafers. Yet, knowing him as she did, Jessie had no doubt that the shoes were Gucci, the slacks Calvin Klein and the shirt Ralph Lauren. Dan wore his wealth as he did his clothes—with understated style.

"Hello, Dan," she said, without a smile of greeting.

"Hello, Jessica. How have you been?" Like everything else about him, his manner toward his former wife was flawless. Until he was crossed.

Jessie regarded his forced, three-thousand-dollar smile and squelched the unwanted memory of another man's slightly crooked front tooth. She dropped her gaze and took a drink of the now-cool coffee before answering. "I'm fine. You?"

"Great!" he said, pushing a degree of enthusiasm into his voice and attitude. "Acapulco was wonderful."

The mention of his Mexican holiday brought the budding of something that resembled fear to Jessie's fast-beating heart. The trip had been much more than just a vacation for Dan. It had been a honeymoon. Francine, his fiancée of six months, was now his new wife and Cissy's stepmother. A stepmother who would be there when Cissy visited her father on the weekends. A woman who, by Dan's smug admission, was happy to be a wife and homemaker. Francine would be there to provide full-time mothering for Cissy, something he had indicated by inference on more than one occasion that she, Jessie, couldn't do.

"How is Francine?" she asked with a semblance of pleasance, her chin climbing a fraction.

"She's fine. Settling in very nicely." The barest hint of challenge glimmered in Dan's blue eyes that were so much like their daughter's. "We wondered if we could keep Celeste for a week or so, sort of give her and Francine some time to really get to know one another."

Jessie's first reaction to the innocuous question was to scream a firm denial. She already begrudged Dan the time he spent with Cissy, even though she knew she shouldn't. She certainly didn't want a strange woman imposing another set of rules and values on the child. But more than anything, she didn't want to share Cissy's love. The bud of fear in Jessie's breast blossomed. Francine was everything she wasn't. Which was exactly why she couldn't afford to rock this particular boat.

Fighting back her natural impulse, she urged a stilted smile to her lips and said, "Sure. Why not?"

The surprise on Dan's face was quickly replaced with an awkward smile of his own. "Francine is really looking forward to getting to know Celeste. She bought her a lot of things on the trip."

Things! The woman was going to try to buy Cissy's affections! Jessie saw red. Cutting her gaze to his, she said, "That's nice, Dan, but I won't have Cissy spoiled. Besides, Francine should realize you can't buy a child's love."

An angry flush stained her ex-husband's freshly-shaved cheeks. "I'm sure buying Celeste's love is the farthest thing from Francine's mind. She's very good with children. Patient, caring—"

"Spare me," Jessie interrupted rudely, waving her Styrofoam cup through the air and pinning him with a jaded glare. "I know what you're trying to say, Dan. I got the picture loud and clear a few months back. Fran is everything I'm not. Perfection personified. The three-meals-a-day, cookies-and-slippers type."

"You make it sound as if it's a sin to like those things!"

"No, it isn't!" she said, hearing the steady increase in the volume of her voice as she recanted her own position for perhaps the thousandth time. "But neither is it a sin not to live for just those things."

"A woman's place is in the home!" Dan sputtered, his own anger rising. "That's something you wouldn't know about! You spend all your time at the barn with your damned horses!"

Jessie flung the cold coffee to the ground and crushed the cup in her hand. "Your chauvinism is showing, Mr. Givens," she said in a tone that warned him of a temper barely controlled. "And you're one-hundred-percent wrong. I know a lot about it. I spend most of my day at the barn, and then I go home and cook and do laundry and mop floors and bake cookies. I do it all, Dan. It just isn't my favorite thing to do."

"Hey, Jessie!" a loud voice called.

Her head jerked involuntarily toward the sound that came from the track. She waved at the grinning exercise boy riding by on the filly who'd just worked. "Way to go, David! I clocked her at thirty-six!" she called. "See you at the barn!" With a last wave she turned back to Dan, a genuine smile replacing the anger that had contorted her features only a few seconds earlier.

Dan's face wore an expression of patent disbelief. He held up his hand in a weary gesture, amazed as always how anything even remotely connected with the racetrack could bring a smile to her face. "Forget it! There's no talking to you. There never was." He turned to walk away, then turned back. "I'll pick Celeste up here about ten Friday morning."

The momentary pleasure had already fled Jessie's face. "She'll be ready."

She watched Dan walk away and mentally cursed herself for being so obstinate. Seeing him always brought out the worst in her and the terrible part was, little of their trouble had been his fault. Still, he was a constant reminder of her poor judgment, or her blatant disregard for her conscience's warning. She wasn't certain which. She only knew that anger was the only way she could combat the guilt that being with him always made her feel. A guilt that, after so many years, she was beginning to believe would never go away.

Jessie shifted her gaze from the darkened ceiling and raised her head to glance at the glowing red numerals of her digital clock. A quarter to three. Her head dropped to the pillow in tandem with the moan of weary resignation soughing from her lips. Sleep was impossible. Every time she closed her eyes, she saw Dan's glowing face as he extolled Francine's domestic virtues.

There was no doubt about it, Jessie thought, she was running scared. Selfish or not, she didn't want to share Cissy. She smiled wryly at the darkness. Wouldn't Dan be surprised to find that she actually needed something besides work and horses in her life?

With a sigh of frustration, she threw back the sheet and padded barefoot into the kitchen of her trailer. She flipped on the venthood light and rummaged around in the spice cabinet for the aspirin she used when little aches and pains kept her awake. Tonight she needed them. Or something a lot stronger. Somehow, she didn't think aspirin could ease this particular pain. Recapping the bottle, she popped three tablets into her mouth, downed them with a glass of tap water, then stood with her head leaning against the cabinets, hating the thought of going back to the rumpled, frustration-tossed bed.

Instead, she unlocked the sliding-glass door that opened onto a small deck at the back and went outside. A silvery slice of moon hung low in the sky and the Milky Way spilled across the heavens. The mournful hooting of an owl from the wooded area beyond the trailer park sounded loud in the dark quiet.

Jessie eased into a lawn chair and propped her feet on the patio table of expanded metal. At least out here there was a feeling of peace. Maybe if she got lucky, some of it would rub off on her. She slid lower in the chair and leaned her head against the back with a sigh of defeat as the inexorable memories swept through her. Memories of the mistakes she'd made that had brought her to this point. Mistakes that started when she'd turned down Bodie Lattimer's proposal because of the foolish pride and insecurities she'd inherited from her mother.

Bodie.

She sighed. She'd let him go six years ago, after convincing herself that what they shared wasn't love, but a blazing sexual attraction that would eventually burn itself out. She'd tried to make him see that marriage to him would set her in the shadow of his steadily rising career, and tie her down until she couldn't pursue her own dream of becoming the best woman trainer in the country.

And she had let him go because her mother had filled her mind with reminders of what her father had done and had made her believe that Bodie would treat her the same way.

As a child, Jessie had always listened avidly when her mother told her how she'd met and married Merle Harper. She could recount the tale by rote... everything that had led up to their divorce when she, Jessie, was three.

She had never seen her father in the flesh, but as she'd grown up his picture frequented the newspapers, where he was portrayed as one of Florida's most prominent and prestigious sons. The solemn likeness portrayed with paper and ink was much more flattering than the picture of him painted by a biased Vera. As much as she loved her mother, Jessie found it hard to believe that anyone who looked as miserable and forlorn as her father did in his pictures could be all bad, just as it was hard for her to believe that Bodie Lattimer would have treated her in the same way if she'd followed the urgings of her heart and married him. And yet, for reasons that didn't seem so important now, she'd let him go and rebounded right into a situation with Dan that, ironically, almost paralleled her parents' marriage.

Jessie shifted in the lawn chair and blinked back the stinging heat gathering beneath her eyelids.

She'd met Dan Givens soon after Bodie had packed up and left for parts unknown, when, feeling more lonely, unattractive and unsure of herself than she ever had, she'd begun to play the flirt. It was funny that the problems in her life had all started just because she'd wanted to try to make Dan fall for her. She still remembered how she'd planned and campaigned for his attention, just as a candidate campaigned for public office. She still recalled her surprise—and everyone else's—when he'd proposed to her within three months. And she could never forget that she'd married Dan, even with Vera's warnings ringing in her ears, in the first totally impulsive move she'd ever made. Her life hadn't been the same since.

Jessie sat brooding at the night. What was the matter with her, anyway? With the new threat of losing Cissy uppermost in her mind, she began to look closely at herself, determined to be truthful, even brutal, about her failed relationships.

She knew their failing had something to do with who she thought she was and how she felt about herself. It had been Vera's prodding and her own pride and driving ambition that had kept her from working things out with Bodie, but her relationship with Dan had failed for totally different reasons. Dan had wanted and expected things from her that she just wasn't willing to give...because she hadn't loved him enough.

You didn't really love him at all.

"No!" She spoke aloud, the word racing unexpectedly through her mind. Her body, relaxed in the lawn chair, jerked simultaneously in shock. Her fingers gripped its arms. She wanted to run from the unwanted mental accusation, wanted to follow the vocal and vehement denial that echoed and disappeared through the silence of the night.

Jessie willed herself to relax. It wasn't true. She would never have married someone she didn't believe she cared about. *Believe.* That was the catch, she thought, as things began to crystallize in her mind for the first time. She had *believed* she loved Dan, had worked very hard at convincing herself of it. But believing hadn't made it so. For the first time, she realized that this was the root of her guilt over Dan. Their marriage hadn't worked because she hadn't married him for the right reasons. She'd married him in an effort to find a replacement for Bodie. She should have known that was impossible.

She dropped her head in her hands, willing the memories to go away. She didn't want to think about Bodie, yet memories of her marriage to Dan invariably brought them. And she knew she could no more stop those memories than she could stop the sun from coming up in the east every morning ... or put an end to Vera's bitterness, which had spilled over into her own life and helped destroy what she and Bodie had shared.

Beep, beep, beep, beep. The sudden sound of the alarm pulled Jessie's tormented thoughts from the past. Bolting from the lawn chair, she ran into the bedroom to shut it off before it woke Cissy.

Cissy. Her own daughter. Her own mistake.

Of their own volition, Jessie's bare feet headed toward the child's room. Moonlight seeped through a crack in the curtains, gilding the back of her daughter's blond head. Jessie reached out and touched the soft, fine hair. A pang of love so sharp it was physically painful stabbed her heart. She loved Cissy so much. Couldn't imagine loving her more. Yet sometimes when her memories of Bodie pulled her into a vortex of longing and stirred the waters of uncertainty about where she was heading with her life, she wondered what it would be like to have him for her husband and Cissy's father.

Heaving a sigh of regret for the past, she left the room to dress for the day. She dreaded, as always, disturbing Cissy's rest to take her to the track, where she would curl up on a cot in the tack room and sleep until the sounds of the stirring racetrack woke her. She dreaded another day of facing the problems that her night of wakefulness failed to solve.

It was quite possibly the longest day of her life, Jessie thought as she went about her work. The nagging, ultra-hot May day had joined forces with her sleepless night, and the weight of the two was draining her usual vitality.

To make matters worse, an owner had come in to watch his horse run the day before, and he wasn't too thrilled over the fact that it had run next to last. Now it looked as if he were so angry he was going to give the horse to someone else to train.

Angrily, she slapped a blob of mud onto the bottom of a horse's hoof. She and Vera were a small operation and needed all the horses they could get. It wasn't fair that they had to suffer because the owner wanted to see his horse run and they were forced to enter it in a race it hadn't had a shot to win. They shouldn't have to pay for the whims of an owner. They'd done a good job on the colt . . .

Tied up in the fury of her thoughts, she didn't hear the approaching footsteps over the sound of the fan that blew directly into the gelding's stall. She didn't see the smile that lifted the corners of a thick, dark mustache and spread with slow satisfaction across the man's ruggedly masculine features . . . didn't know he was within a thousand miles until he spoke.

"I swear, woman, you've still got the sweetest rear end this side of the Mississippi."

Chapter Two

The words, those softly rumbled words delivered in that deep gravelly bass that was so achingly familiar, halted the hands packing mud onto the horse's hoof and brought Jessie's heartbeats to a screeching whoa.

Bodie.

She drew in a deep breath. He was back. Several things scampered more or less at once through her whirling mind. First, she was bent over, facing the back of the stall, "the sweetest rear end this side of the Mississippi" facing the doorway. Second, she was hot, sweaty and probably didn't smell like a rose. Third, what in sweet hell was Bodie Lattimer doing here, anyway? Now, of all times—when her life needed fewer complications, not more. She slapped a page torn from an old condition book onto the gelding's mudded hoof, uncertain how best to greet him after so long.

Finally she dropped the horse's leg and straightened to her full five feet nine inches. Only seconds had passed, but it seemed like eons since she'd heard him speak. Her eyes betrayed none of her uncertainty as she turned to face him, automatically straightening her shoulders as her mother always preached, automatically bracing herself for her first really good look at him in years.

Lifting her chin to a degree just shy of haughty, an involuntary defense mechanism against the overwhelming masculinity she knew from experience oozed from every pore of him, she planted her hands on her hips and raked him with a slow, scorching look.

He looked, she thought with a sinking heart, fantastic.

He stood with one shoulder resting against the cement door frame, his arms akimbo, the oxford cloth of his pale blue, monogrammed shirt straining against his massive shoulders. The sleeves were rolled up, revealing forearms lightly sprigged with dark hair. Arms that were pure brawn from holding fifteen-hundred-pound horses with nothing but a twitch in one hand while "floating," or filing, their teeth with a rasp with the other. His shirt was tucked neatly into well-worn Wranglers that clung to his thighs and adhered to his slim hips and the bulge of his manhood with heart-stopping intimacy. The bulk of his two hundred or so pounds rested on his left leg, and his right was crossed in front of it, the toe of his boot digging into the red dirt and straw.

The six years had been kind to him, she thought, willing her heart to a steady rhythm. He was still as fit as he ever was. But it wasn't just his body that looked good to her. There was his face, that rugged face with the piercing, loden-green eyes shadowed by long lashes and heavy brows; the vibrant, tobacco brown of his hair, a little grayer now than the last time she'd seen him, and the bold slash of his nose that looked a bit too big without the luxuriant mustache he sported beneath it. His mouth was—had always been—incredibly sexy to Jessie. Right now it bore a small cut on his lower lip.

He gave her a slow smile; instant, fanlike crinkles appeared at the corners of his eyes. "Damn, but you look good, girl," he said in that husky, sexy voice.

Her pulse accelerated, and she realized she'd lost control of her heartbeats after all. Just as she had so many years ago, she was responding to the man so close to her. And just as she'd known then, she was realizing all over again that he was still a threat to her heart.

She looked down at her less than clean Levi's and her rumpled, sweat-stained shirt. She could feel her hair, snatched back earlier into a haphazard ponytail, straggling around her heat-flushed face. She wanted to believe him...needed to. Bodie had always made her feel pretty, special, more a woman. But right this minute, she looked a mess and knew it.

Her mama was right. You couldn't trust any man. Besides, she was still smarting over her encounter with Dan. "And you're as full of it as you ever were, Bodie Lattimer," she drawled with a wry twist of her lips.

Giving him her back, she bent to retrieve her box of grooming tools.

"Need any help?" he asked.

When she favored him with another go-to-hell look, Bodie's smile broadened. All of a sudden, the stall was much too small. She headed a determined course toward the doorway. He straightened, his eyes never leaving hers. When she would have stepped through the door, his arm shot out and blocked her exit.

Jessie forced her breathing to normalcy. Her gaze meandered with insolent deliberation from the crisp, black hair peeking from the vee of his shirt, up the tanned column of his neck and over his deeply grooved cheeks. She stared up at him, her eyes filled with a disdain she was far from feeling. "Stop playing games, Bodie."

His smile faded. His voice was low as he murmured, "Oh, but I'm not, sweetheart."

Why did she imagine it sounded like a threat? Jessie's facade of insouciance cracked. So did her voice. "Why are you back, Bodie? What do you want?"

"You." His answer was short and, as Bodie usually was, to the point. It was also blessedly, heartbreakingly sweet. For even though the seriousness of that deep, raspy statement brought fear into Jessie's heart, it also started a fierce exultation pounding in her bloodstream.

"You must've been smoking your socks again, Lattimer," she began, trying to duck under his arm, determined not to let him know the effect he had on her. "There's no way I—"

Her scathing tirade was cut off as he lowered his arm and scooped her close, the sudden movement knocking the grooming tools from her hands. Past experience reminded her that struggling would be an exercise in futility. Jessie's movements stilled.

She stared mutely into his eyes, vowing she wouldn't fight him. Warm hands moved to her shoulders. Their gazes meshed—warm brown to daring green—then his head tilted a few degrees to one side and began a slow descent. When his mouth was a heartbeat from its destination, she jerked her head sideways. The kiss grazed her cheek.

Immediately he moved his hand up, grasping her chin between his thumb and callused fingers. His mouth swooped, taking hers in a bruising kiss that drove all thought of resistance from her mind. She felt the sweep of his mustache abrading her flesh as his hard, hungry mouth feasted on hers. Without conscious thought, Jessie parted her lips, inviting the invasion of his tongue. She wasn't disappointed. The proprietorial thrusting triggered a reciprocal hunger she remembered only too well as something she'd never had much control over.

His hands slid from her shoulders to her hips. Bodie rammed his hands into the back pockets of her jeans and, cupping her rounded bottom, drew her more deeply into the web of desire binding them together. A whimper hung in her throat and her hands inched upward from her sides to cling to the lifeline of his belt loops.

The sound seemed to break the spell, and he began to pull away from her. First his tongue left the warm cavity of her mouth, then his hands moved from her pockets to rest at her waist. His mouth gentled before he took his lips from hers, returning almost reluctantly for a succession of light, nibbling kisses.

"Hello, Jessie," he whispered.

"Bodie..." She spoke against the lips that then forsook hers for a moment to place moist kisses to her cheek and ear. "Why are you doing this?" she groaned, throwing her head back to meet his eyes.

"Seemed like a good idea at the time," he said with a lopsided smile. Reaching out one long finger, he looped a tendril of fair hair behind her ear.

Jessie shut her eyes and tried to gather her diffuse emotions. Anger warred with guilt; fury fought with an almost overwhelming desire. And her irritation over his sudden, unannounced reappearance in her life was dissipating under the pure joy she felt at seeing him again. Somehow she had to regain control of her emotions. Her lashes lifted; her eyes probed his. "Be serious, Bodie."

"I am. Dead serious."

Another flicker of unease whipped through her. "And just what does that cryptic statement mean?"

"It means, Jessica Lorene, that I let you get away from me once, and I'm not going to let that happen again."

All the blood drained from Jessie's head, leaving her pale and light-headed, while her heart felt full to bursting point. Her eyes drifted shut and she swayed into him. His hands tightened on her waist.

"Look at me, Jessie," he commanded, lifting her chin with the knuckles of one hand. The thick, dark fringe of her lashes rose. "I should never have let it end the way it did six years ago."

Her heart breaking all over again at the remembered pain of his leaving and the reasons leading up to it lent a huskiness to her voice. "That's the only way it could have ended."

He shook his head. "I don't think so. And I don't intend to let it happen this time."

This time. He really did intend to come back into her life. She couldn't bear it if he did . . . couldn't bear it if he didn't. But nothing had changed. She still had her dreams, and even if she lost sight of them from time to time, they didn't include a man—especially not one as supremely confident as Bodie Lattimer.

"There isn't going to be a 'this time,' Bodie," she said, pushing against the solid wall of his body in an effort to put some physical and emotional distance between them.

He let her go and, as if they were talking about nothing more important than the weather, stooped to gather the scattered tools. She watched while the tanned hands with the light dusting of hair on their tops and the fingers scored with white welts of scars from the sharp edges of the teeth he worked on quickly brought order to the hoof pick, alcohol, brushes and other grooming tools housed in the plastic carrier. Still he didn't speak.

Shifting from one foot to the other, Jessie glared down at the muscles shifting beneath his shirt. How did you argue with someone who wouldn't even talk? she asked herself testily. She wanted to reach out and grab that thick, dark head of hair and shake him until his teeth rattled. He had no right to come back and upset her world. No right to come strolling into her shedrow as if they hadn't had the fight to end all fights six years ago. And he damn sure had no right to kiss her, especially when he hadn't come close enough to even speak to her the few times he had been in town.

Jessie's breathing quickened, her color rising along with her anger. There wasn't going to be a next time. She meant it. He had no right to come back here and just expect—

Her thoughts skittered to an abrupt halt when he stood and held out the tools, his eyes boring into hers. Automatically, her hands reached for the box. She opened her mouth to tell him to get the hell away from her barn and her life, but the next words from his lips stopped her.

"About that next time…you're dead wrong, Jess." The surprising, uncompromising statement was delivered in a tone that brooked no arguments, gave no quarter. Then he turned on the heels of his battered boots and walked away.

Stunned speechless, Jessie watched him go, surprise holding her mouth agape, fury fizzling to an impotent sizzle and an ache she couldn't put into words squeezing her heart.

Bodie forced one foot in front of the other, oblivious to anything except the need to put as much distance between himself and Jessie as he could. A bead of perspiration trickled down his back that had nothing to do with the fact that it was barely eleven o'clock and the contrary Shreveport-Bossier City temperature had already reached a record-breaking high for the middle of May. He was flat-out nervous.

What had come over him back there—grabbing her and kissing her like that? Knowing Jess, it was a wonder she hadn't slapped fire from him. And even worse, he'd as much as told her he intended to pick up where they'd left off six years ago.

Way to go, Lattimer. Don't try to charm the lady— just run over her like a steamroller. He snorted in wry amusement. No woman in her right mind would go for that kind of treatment. Especially one as independent as Jessie.

He reached the stable gate, waved at the guard and headed toward the Bronco, trying to erase the memory of the kiss and the feel of her in his arms.

It had felt right to hold her, he thought, unlocking the door. She was tall enough that it didn't put a crimp in his neck to kiss her, and short enough that he felt protective. She'd felt so soft and womanly, so curvy and sexy, and her mouth had opened to him, just as it always had. Did that mean she was still interested?

Fool! He cranked the ignition and pulled onto the blacktop road that ran parallel to the east side of the racetrack. What it meant was that Jessie had a healthy, natural sex drive. He wanted to believe it was more. He wanted to believe that she still loved him, just as she used to. He needed to believe it because no one else had ever come close to taking her place in his heart.

He heaved a deep, disgusted breath. She was everything he wanted in a woman, yet he'd let her get away from him . . . let Vera outtalk him. He'd wanted to die when Jessie had turned him down and then married someone else a few months later.

It had taken a while, but he'd put her from his mind—most of the time. Yet sometimes, when he was at his most lonely and vulnerable, the memories returned to haunt him, just as they had the night he decided to come back and make her his. He realized once and for all he would never be really happy until he had her in his life again. He'd let her get away once, but just as he'd told her a few minutes earlier, it wouldn't happen again.

Not this time.

Weariness tugged at Jessie with invisible fingers, pulling a sigh from her as she placed the last slice of cheese on the hamburgers sizzling on the charcoal grill. Cissy wanted grilled hamburgers and, other than the trouble she usually had starting the charcoal, it had seemed like a good idea to Jessie, especially after the day she'd been through. At least she wouldn't have a grease-spattered stove to clean up, she thought, letting her thoughts return with reluctance to the man who, along with Dan, was doing such a great job disrupting her life.

She took a sip of her iced tea and favored the world at large with a wry smile. Darn Bodie, anyway! Actually, she'd held her own pretty well, even though he'd caught her off guard. She wondered just what he would do to further the relationship he'd promised her they would have again—not that it would do any good, whatever it was. Unwanted, a memory of the kiss they'd shared sauntered through her mind. She groaned aloud. Her emotions were so mixed up she felt as if they'd been put in a paper sack and shaken up. She sighed again, disgusted anew at her reaction to his kiss, and resolutely forced the incident from her mind.

A quick glance assured her that the hamburgers were ready, and she turned to scan the neighboring yards for her daughter. Cissy and three other kids were about four trailer spaces over, walking along the edge of the wooded area that bordered the park, their heads bent, obviously inspecting something on the ground. Jessie hated living in a trailer park because she didn't like being so close to her neighbors, but at least there was no lack of companions for Cissy. And in all honesty, the park wasn't so bad, especially since their spot had a view out back.

Putting her index and little finger in her mouth, Jessie cut loose with a shrill whistle. From somewhere deep in her mind came the memory of Dan's frown of disapproval when she'd lapsed into what he termed her "unladylike behavior." As soon as the sound penetrated the sultry air Cissy whirled and began to run home. A perverse sort of smile curved Jessie's lips. Unladylike or not, the whistle usually got action.

Cissy arrived at the redwood deck with blond wisps of hair straggling from her braids. She pushed the hair from her bright blue eyes, excitement molding her gamine features. "Mom, David found some coyote tracks!"

Jessie plucked up the buns with her fingers, swearing under her breath at the heat. "He did? Where?"

"Really," Cissy said with a nod, her eyes wide. "Down by the woods. He says we can get his brother to set a trap and catch it!"

Visions of some poor neighborhood dog—probably the culprit who had left the tracks—ensnared in a trap, flashed through Jessie's mind. She didn't know if David's big brother would set the trap or not, but... "Hmm," she said, squirting some ketchup on a bun.

"Did you ever think about what you'd do if you caught a coyote?"

If possible, Cissy's eyes widened even more.

Jessie's gaze probed her daughter's with serious intensity. "Who's gonna get him out of the trap if you catch him?"

Cissy looked uncomfortable and shrugged her shoulders.

"And what if someone's dog got in it instead of the coyote and got its leg broken?" Jessie had found out as soon as the child was old enough to start communicating that it was better to show both sides of an issue rather than tell her outright she couldn't do something. That's when she'd invented their "what-if" game. So far it had worked amazingly well. She put a slice of tomato on the hamburger and plopped on the top of the bun, waiting for a reaction. She could almost see the thoughts turning in Cissy's mind.

"You mean like Scruffy?"

"Yes."

"I wouldn't like that," Cissy said with a shake of her blond head.

"Neither would Mr. Jones."

"I'd better go tell David after supper," Cissy said suddenly. "Can I, Mom?"

"Sure," Jessie told her with a grin, setting Cissy's plate on the small table and pulling her kid-size lawn chair up to it. "Here you go. One hamburger with cheese, tomato and lots of ketchup."

"Thanks, Mom."

Jessie fixed her own burger, then sat down in a lawn chair, her paper plate on her lap, thinking about the what-if game while she ate. What if she had married

Bodie all those years ago? What would she be doing
with her life now? Would there be other children?
Would she still be training horses? Would they still be
as happy as she remembered them being? And what if
her father hadn't been so weak? What if her mother
hadn't been so strong? Unfortunately, there were no
ready answers to her questions. Maybe, she reasoned,
the game only worked for children.

She and Cissy were just finishing when the sound of
a truck pulling into the front drive interrupted the
comparative quiet of the summer evening.

"Granny's coming!" Cissy exclaimed, her sensitive ears picking up the truck's unique sound.

Jessie closed her eyes. She wasn't certain she could
handle Vera right now. Not after everything else the
day had offered.

They heard the truck door slam and, in a matter of
seconds, Vera Harper, dressed in crisply starched jeans
and a short-sleeved knit shirt that showed off her well-
preserved figure to advantage, rounded the side of the
trailer. Her hair, still dark, had an attractive silver
streak just off center, and her classic, shoulder-length
bob was held at the nape of her neck with a piece of
navy-blue grosgrain ribbon. Her face was relatively
unlined, and the only thing marring her otherwise
good looks was the pinched tightness around her
mouth.

Jessie couldn't help but think what a waste those
looks were. Despite the interest they generated, her
mother never opened herself up for anything but the
most casual and cool relationships with the opposite
sex, a fact that always filled Jessie with a sense of
sadness. Even though her own past performances with

men weren't too great, she had at least given it her best shot.

Jessie forced a smile to her lips. "Hello, Mother. Had dinner?"

"I ate in town," Vera said, climbing the three steps to the deck and sinking onto the webbed lounge chair. Cissy promptly crawled up into her grandmother's lap and planted a ketchupy kiss on one cheek. Vera smiled and snuggled Cissy closer.

One thing about her mother, Jessie thought, was that she'd never held the fact that she knew Jessie was making a mistake in marrying Dan against the child who had come from that union. A fool could see that the adoration between Cissy and her grandmother was mutual.

"I talked to Bodie Lattimer this afternoon," Vera said without preamble.

Jessie responded with a slight smile. Just like Bodie, Vera jumped into the conversation with both feet. They had more in common than either one realized.

"Did you?"

Vera nodded. "I hear he stopped by to see you. Why didn't you tell me?"

Jessie stared into her mother's accusing eyes a moment before looking at Cissy's ketchup-smeared face. The child didn't need to hear this. Smiling at her daughter, she said, "Why don't you go wash your face and then tell David not to let his brother set the trap?"

"Okay!" Cissy scrambled from her grandmother's lap, her eager legs carrying her inside.

"What's this about a trap?" Vera queried, a frown drawing her dark eyebrows together.

"Nothing, Mother." The two women stared at each other in a familiar clash of wills. Clashes that had become more and more frequent—and over everything from how she was raising Cissy to how to do up a horse—since Bodie walked out of Jessie's life. "I didn't tell you because I knew you'd do just what you're doing."

"And just what am I doing?" Vera asked with a lift of her brows.

"Giving me the third degree, just like you did when I was sixteen. But I'm not sixteen, Mother. I'm thirty. And I don't owe you any blow-by-blow account of what goes on during my days. Or my nights, either, for that matter," she tacked on without thought.

"It sounds as though you might have upcoming plans for your nights," Vera observed dryly.

Jessie leaped to her feet and began clearing up the debris left from the meal. "I'm not even going to comment on that."

"He's a rambler, Jessie."

"I know that!" Jessie glanced up from screwing on the mustard lid, determined to hold her own with her mother. "How do you know if Bodie is even interested in a relationship with me?"

"Carson's groom saw him kissing you." The statement was made with the triumphant assurance of a poker player holding four aces.

It was Jessie's turn to look embarrassed. Cissy came out of the trailer, threw a "Bye, Mom," over her shoulder and raced down the steps and across the yard. Jessie hardly noticed. She should have known someone would see that kiss. It was probably all over the backside by now. Damn Bodie Lattimer, anyway! She lifted her chin. "It was just a hello kiss."

"Was it? Can you honestly tell me you wouldn't like to pick up where the two of you left off?"

Jessie turned away, slammed the lid to the grill down, then turned back to face her mother. Her fingers twisted together. "No. As a matter of fact, I can't. But that's impossible. We're not the same two people. I'm not an easily swayed twenty-four anymore. Back then, what you thought was best for me outweighed everything else."

Vera's mouth turned down at the corners. "What do you mean, what I thought was best for you?"

"I mean that if you'd kept your nose out of it, things might have been different. I might have married him. I still remember feeling like a wishbone—torn between what Bodie wanted, what I thought I wanted and your theory on the problems I'd have if I did marry him."

Vera pushed herself to her feet, suppressed anger simmering in her dark eyes. "And where do you think you'd be by now if I *hadn't* stuck my nose in? I know his type. He likes his beer and his women. If you had married him you'd have a couple of kids and be divorced by now."

A look of disbelief tautened Jessie's features. She began to laugh. Softly. Sadly. Tears started in her brown eyes. She sobered abruptly and, wearing a weary smile, faced her mother once more.

"Oh, Mother," she whispered, "in case you haven't noticed, and with the exception of the number of kids—that's just where I am now. And I got there without Bodie Lattimer."

Chapter Three

Louisiana Downs sat on a piece of land wedged between Highway Eighty and Interstate Twenty. A thoroughly modern facility, it faced east, its solid glass front offering racing fans an unobliterated view of the racetrack, the infield and a lean strip of wooded area that hid a meandering bayou.

The backside hugged the interstate, its barn area laid out in rows from A to D, with each barn numbered. Jessie and Vera were stabled in D-4, near the stable gate and the receiving barn, which housed horses who didn't have stalls on the track and were brought in from nearby farms on the day they were to race.

As usual, the barn area was humming, but Jessie was oblivious to everything but the fact that it was Friday and Dan would be there to pick Cissy up at any time. No one seeing her bustle around the shedrow—

all business and confidence—could ever have known she'd silently cried herself to sleep in a chair beside her daughter's bed the night before.

They couldn't have possibly known with how much reluctance she had packed enough of Cissy's clothes for a week, or how lovingly she had added Mary Elizabeth, a bedraggled Cabbage Patch Kid who wore a stoic smile. Then, in typical Jessie fashion, she had plastered a smile that matched Mary Elizabeth's to her lips and set about making the best of the day, which was hard, considering she hadn't seen Bodie since he'd arrived without warning three days earlier.

As the morning wore on, Jessie had sent Cissy to the other side of the barn to visit with friends, which she hoped would keep her out of trouble. She was topping off the last water bucket, her mind filled with both how she would act when Dan and Francine arrived and what she would do when Bodie decided to show up again, when he sauntered back into her troubled world.

"That colt is dropping a lot of feed."

Her eyes jerked from the water bucket to the man standing near her tack room door wearing a blood-spattered shirt and a heart-stopping smile. Bodie. The wondering and waiting for him to show up again were over. A sense of anticipation warred with a feeling of something uncomfortably akin to fear, which was silly. She had nothing to fear from Bodie Lattimer. Nothing.

His grooved cheeks were freshly shaven and the faint scent of something peppery and masculine wafted to her on a barely perceptible breeze. A royal-blue baseball cap with a cartoon picture of a horse whose wide-open smile showed a mouthful of shockingly large teeth and the words Lattimer Equine Dentistry stamped in white was pulled down to shade his face.

Jessie drew in a deep breath. There ought to be a law banning men exuding sexuality in the quantities Bodie did. As usual, her heart scampered to catch up with her breathing and, to combat the unwanted awareness, she sought refuge in anger.

Why did he finally have to come when her face showed the ravages of the past few days and her sleepless nights? Why had he picked the day Dan and Francine might show up at any time? And, darn it, why, after telling her he intended to pick up where they had left off so many years ago, was he talking business? She knew the colt was dropping feed. He'd also drifted into the outside rail when he'd breezed earlier that morning.

Favoring him with a scorching look, she eased the pressure off the spray nozzle of the water hose. "I know he is."

Bodie, unmoved by her coolness, stood with his bare arms folded across his chest, his hands tucked beneath his armpits. His biceps bulged from the knit bands of the shirt sleeves. His booted feet were spread in an easy, confident stance, and his face held a look that, if she didn't know him so well, could almost pass for innocence as he asked, "Had his teeth worked on lately?"

"Jamison did them just before we claimed him," Jessie supplied.

"Jamison doesn't use a mouth jack. You can't work on those back teeth as well without one."

"I know," she said testily, favoring him with a long-suffering look. "You've told me often enough."

A smile crinkled the corners of his eyes and hiked up one corner of his mouth. "Yeah. I guess I have, at that." He jerked his head in the direction of the colt. "Want me to take a look? My tools are just around the corner."

He *was* going to talk business. Part of her was relieved; part of her wanted to heave a sigh of disappointment. Still, she didn't want him around when Dan came.

"Today isn't a good day."

"Why not?"

"It just isn't," she snapped.

Bodie knew she was stalling him for some reason. He shrugged. "If you don't let me get him today, I'm not sure when I can get around to it."

She didn't doubt it. Everyone on the track would want to avail themselves of his expertise while he was around, before he took off again as unexpectedly as he'd come. She sighed. The horse did need the work. Maybe if she let him do it he would go away and leave her alone. He was fast. He could be finished in just a little while, surely before Dan and Francine arrived.

"Okay. Do him. But make it quick, huh?"

He only smiled and reached to pull the bill of the cap down over his eyes. "I'll go get the Bronco."

Bodie was back in a matter of minutes, and Jessie held the horse while he unloaded his stainless-steel bucket of rasps and filled the bucket with fresh water, adding a generous dollop of antiseptic. Then he entered the colt's stall and loosened the halter enough that the horse could open his mouth wider and there was less chance of the tools hanging up. When he started to insert the mouth jack, the colt threw his head and shied backward.

"Whoa, now," Bodie murmured patiently, his deep voice drawing Jessie's attention to his mouth. Rubbing the horse's head and ears with strong, confident hands and murmuring soothingly all the while, he eased the leather straps up and over the horse's ears and inserted the metal part of the speculum into his mouth.

A shiver of longing tripped down Jessie's spine when she remembered that same voice whispering patient words of praise and encouragement in her ear while she searched out all the ways to please him. Forcing her mind from the sensuous turn of her thoughts and the random realization that his lip had almost healed, she offered belatedly, "He's a little head-shy."

The grooves at the corners of Bodie's mouth deepened. "Thanks."

She watched as he filled a large, stainless-steel syringe with the antiseptic mixture and squirted it in the colt's mouth, a process he continued until it was washed clean. Then he reached inside and, with fingers sensitized to myriad problems, began a thorough check of the upper jaw. Even when he was actually floating, or filing the teeth with a rasp, he could carry on an eye-to-eye conversation. It had never ceased to amaze her that ninety-five percent of the work he did on a horse's mouth was done by touch instead of sight.

And ninety-five percent of his loving is done the same way.

He grinned suddenly, bringing her wandering mind back into line. Embarrassment for being caught with her thoughts down sent hot color rushing to her cheeks. She was thankful that his attention was still fixed on the colt's problem, even though his eyes were on her.

His hand emerged from the yawning cavity with the equivalent of a baby tooth between his fingers. "He's shedding caps. This one was ready to fall out. You'd probably have found it in his feed tub or water bucket in a day or two."

Jessie nodded, turning her attention to the problem at hand as he extended his examination to the lower jaw. Caps were a familiar problem. So, she thought, were unwanted erotic memories.

She watched as he peered into the horse's mouth for a brief visual inspection, then shrugged. "That's about it, except for a few places in the back. I'll smooth things out and he'll be good as new."

He tossed the cap into the bucket of tools and reached for a rasp, completely unaware of Jessie's discomfiture. She exhaled a soft burst of air. All business.

The touch-up didn't take long, but even so, Jessie managed to get her wayward feelings under control. As she watched him work with quick efficiency, a certain pride built within her at the care he took. Watching him made her aware of why he was considered the best.

When he finished with the final comment, "Smooth as a baby's bottom," they turned the colt free and Jessie followed him out into the shedrow. Wearing a slight smile of satisfaction, he set the bucket of tools on the tack box, took the blue cap from his sweat-dampened head and tossed it onto a bale of alfalfa near the stall door. He wiped his perspiring face on his shirt-sleeves, then went to the hose and sprayed a light film of water onto his face and arms.

What would happen now? she wondered, leaning self-consciously against the barn wall. Now that he'd finished his work, would he return the conversation to them? What would he do?

"Did you cut yourself?"

The innocent question interrupted Jessie's thoughts and brought her back to the reality of the day with abrupt rudeness. Her startled eyes flew to Cissy, who was holding a cup full of crushed ice, then to Bodie, who was looking down at the child and comparing her obvious likeness to Jessie with a dawning comprehension. As always, his nearness had pushed everything and everyone from her mind—including the fact that Cissy had been visiting on the other side of the barn.

Bodie's eyes, filled with an unmistakable reproach, found hers. *She could have been mine...*

A sense of sadness blanketed her heart. He was right. Cissy could have been his. Should have been.

Shifting his gaze from Jessie to his bloodstained shirt, he shook his head and answered the waiting child. "No. I've been pulling teeth."

"Are you a dentist?" Cissy asked, a wary expression in her blue eyes.

"Yes. A horse dentist."

Cissy pondered the statement, a frown marring her smooth brow. "What's your name?" she asked, realizing she hadn't seen him before. "Did you just move here?"

He regarded the pint-size version of Jessie who stood looking at him with the same confidence molding her tiny features that he'd seen so often on her mother's face. His heart constricted and his gaze softened. She was so much like Jessie it hurt to look at her.

"My name is Bodie, and yes, I've just moved back. I used to live here a long time ago, before you were born. And your name is…?" He let the sentence trail off in question.

"Celeste Aimee Givens," she offered with a touch of pomp. "My daddy and Francine, she's my new mommie," she explained, "are coming to get me in a minute. They went to Mexico and brought me lots of presents!"

Bodie didn't miss the way the color drained from Jessie's face when Cissy referred to Francine as her new mommie. Sympathetic pain flooded him. "That's great!" he told her with forced enthusiasm. "Really great!"

Cissy, deciding that the stranger was properly impressed, tilted her pigtailed head sideways. "Do you do fillings?" she asked suddenly.

"I beg your pardon?" Bodie asked.

"Fillings? In the horses' teeth?" she questioned, opening her own mouth and poking one finger inside to point to a filling of her own.

In spite of himself, Bodie laughed. The sound, plus an appreciative glance at Jessie, sent a thrill of longing for what might have been scampering through her body. Their eyes clung in a sort of desperate searching, emotions superimposing themselves one on top of the other in a montage of changing feelings—love, reproach, a throbbing sexual awareness and a wish that things could have been different. Unfortunately, Jessie thought, too much time had passed, and too much had happened in their lives for there to be any hope of happiness for them.

"Well, do you?" Cissy prompted when it became apparent that the tall man was more interested in looking at her mother than answering her.

In spite of himself, Bodie found his attention drawn back to the child. "No. I'm afraid I don't do fillings. I just pull out the bad teeth."

"I have a loose tooth." She wiggled a front tooth to prove her statement. "The tooth fairy is going to bring me money."

"That's super!" Bodie said, entranced by the miniature version of Jessie and filled again with an acute longing for a child of his own. "How much is she going to leave you? A dollar?"

"Bodie!" Jessie cried.

His laughing eyes met hers, which flashed him an I'm-gonna-get-you-back look.

Cissy frowned up at him. "I don't know. I never lost one before."

"Well, I'd think about it, if I were you," he suggested. He turned to Jessie. "She's a great kid, Jess."

Her irritation at his too-generous tooth fairy offering melted under the warmth of typical maternal pride. "I know. Thank you."

"She takes after her mother."

Jessie raised her eyebrows in question. "Flattery, Bodie?"

"Hell, no, Jess. Just the truth," he rumbled, the look in his eyes vouching for his words.

Her heart fluttering at the candor of his statement and the seriousness of his voice, she asked, "So what brings you back after three days?"

The moment she spoke the words she wanted to call them back. It sounded as if she'd been counting the days since she'd seen him last—which, of course, she had—but she didn't want him to know.

The gleam in his eyes told her he knew exactly what she was thinking. "I came to ask you to have dinner with me tonight."

She shook her head, wanting to say yes, but knowing it was impossible at this point in her life. "I can't."

Bodie leaned against the wall of the barn in much the same pose she'd used before. "Why? It's Friday. Surely Vera lets you off at night. Or," he added as an afterthought, "do you think she'll object to you going out with me?"

Jessie's eyes flashed in warning. "My mother has nothing to say about whom I date."

"Since when?" He couldn't help the sarcasm that crept into his voice.

Sensing the sudden tension in the room, Cissy tugged on her mother's jeans and said, "Mom..."

But before Jessie could do more than flick the child a glance, Bodie relented of his momentary aggravation and reached out to tuck a strand of hair behind Jessie's ear. His fingertips grazed the tender shell and the sensitive spot behind. His thumb rubbed slow, concentric circles over the gold bead piercing the delicate lobe. His eyes spoke of hurt and promise, of pain and pleasure as he growled a soft "Please..."

She looked into his eyes and felt her will dissolving beneath the shimmering green desire reflected there.

Her body swayed toward him; his hand slid around her neck.

"Are you gonna kiss my mom?" Cissy's question burst the fragile feelings building between them. Jessie's lashes fluttered downward to hide her disappointment and Bodie's hand dropped from her neck, leaving the abandoned skin strangely cold.

"No," he said, turning to the child and giving Jessie his strong profile, "I'm not going to kiss your mom. Not this time."

He turned back and placed his finger on Jessie's lips. "Later." The single word was a promise.

"There you are!" The words preceded the tall man and the woman with him who were just rounding the corner of the barn. When the newcomer saw Bodie and Jessie standing so close to one another, he stopped short.

"Daddy!" Cissy squealed, whirling toward the sound of his voice and running to throw herself into his arms.

Even without Cissy's greeting, Bodie would have known who the man was simply by the sudden tautness in Jessie's body. He moved his finger from her lips and turned, extending his hand in greeting, falling easily into the natural confidence that was such a part of his personality.

"Bodie Lattimer," he said, meeting the other man's eyes squarely.

Dan, holding Cissy in one arm and eyeing Bodie's bloodstained clothes with distaste, accepted the handshake with the barest hesitation even as his eyes asked without words who Bodie Lattimer was and what he was doing here. "Dan Givens."

"Nice to meet you," Bodie responded with a pleasant smile.

Jessie stood silently by, watching the exchange. She saw the look on Dan's face. She was familiar with it, had grown accustomed to it. Disapproval. Why, she asked herself again, had Bodie decided to show up today? She knew Dan. He would see Bodie's intimate gesture in the worst possible way and use it as another strike against her.

"Bodie is the horse dentist," she said, hoping to allay Dan's suspicions and failing, if the look in his eyes was anything to go by.

While Jessie worried over how the encounter would affect Dan's already biased view of her, Dan, forced by the very conventions he advocated, turned and ushered his new bride forward. "Francine, you remember Jessie? Mr. Lattimer, my wife, Francine. Francine, Bodie Lattimer."

Jessie nodded in the couple's general direction and Bodie smiled at the petite, dark-haired woman. "Ma'am."

"Hello." Francine, who appeared unaffected by the subtleties of emotion in the room, faced them all with a white, all-American-mom smile. "It's nice to meet you, Mr. Lattimer."

"My pleasure," Bodie murmured, offering her a slow, seductive smile.

Blushing at his blatantly sensual smile, Francine turned to Cissy and held out her arms. Knowing presents were waiting, Cissy went without hesitation from her father's embrace to her new stepmother's arms.

Teeth clenched, Jessie took one step toward them and was halted by Bodie's hand on her shoulder.

Glancing up at him in surprise, she saw the combined tenderness and warning in his eyes. The stiffness left her body; she felt tired, drained. He gave her shoulder a brief, supportive squeeze while Dan watched with unconcealed interest.

"You have a super little girl," Bodie said, hoping to shift Dan's attention from Jessie to his child.

"Yes, she is," Dan agreed stiffly. Then, almost as if he couldn't help himself, he asked, "Have you known Jessica and Celeste long?"

Bodie's eyes rested on Dan's. "I've known Jess a long time," was his cryptic response. "Long before she married."

Jessie saw the considering look on Dan's face. In an effort to end the growing tension by hurrying the threesome off, she spoke to Francine. "I think I have enough clothes packed to do Cissy the week. Her suitcase is in the tack room."

Francine stood with Cissy in her arms, managing, in her vivid-hued sundress, to look cool and feminine even in the humid heat. She looked at Dan. "Will you get it, honey?" When Dan started toward the tack room, she faced Jessie once more. "Washing is no problem. I wash every day."

Of course you do.

"Great," Jessie said weakly.

Silence descended. Jessie looked at the horses tethered to the walking wheel. Watched them make the circle. Twice. She looked from person to person and shifted from one foot to the other. "Look, I hate to be rude," she said at last, "but I really need to get back to work."

Dan, carrying Cissy's suitcase, was just nearing the group. Jessie didn't miss the sudden tightening of his mouth and continued with a false brightness. "Cissy, Mary Elizabeth is in the suitcase."

"And Dr. Seuss?"

"Yes." Facing Francine, Jessie added, "If I've forgotten anything, just give me a call and I can drop it by. There's a notarized letter in the pocket of the suitcase giving you or Dan permission to get treatment for her at the doctor's office if anything were to happen and you couldn't reach me."

A spasm of surprise crossed Dan's face. Francine, impressed with Jessie's thoroughness, responded with lifted brows. Bodie smiled a small half-smile.

"Come give me a kiss, sugar," Jessie said, fighting to keep the huskiness from her voice. Fran lowered Cissy to the floor and the child made a beeline to her mother. Jessie stooped and her arms closed around the small, thin body so tightly that Cissy wriggled to be free. Cradling the child's piquant, freckled face between her palms, Jessie admonished softly, "Be a good girl."

Cissy nodded. Jessie kissed Cissy's cheek. Dan hoisted the suitcase once more and held his hand out toward his daughter.

Blinking rapidly, Jessie watched Cissy place her small hand in Dan's. Jessie's chin angled higher.

"I'll bring her back a week from tomorrow," Dan said.

Jessie nodded in agreement, her teeth clamped tightly on her bottom lip.

Dan turned to Bodie. "Mr. Lattimer."

Bodie responded with a small smile that Dan, already moving down the shedrow, didn't see.

Francine looked at Bodie uncertainly, then turned suddenly toward Jessie. There was a sincerity on her face that couldn't be mistaken. "I'll take good care of her. I promise."

"Coming, Francine?" There was no mistaking the imperious command behind the question.

Francine flicked him a troubled glance. "Yes."

With a last smile at Jessie, she hurried to catch up with Dan and Cissy. Just before they disappeared around the corner of the barn, Cissy turned. "Goodbye, Mr. Bodie," she said with a wave.

"Goodbye, Cissy," he replied with a reciprocal wave before they disappeared from sight. Bodie looked at Jessie, who had begun to bustle around, doing nothing. His heart ached in empathy with her pain. He wanted to go to her and hold her, to tell her everything would be all right, that Cissy would never stop loving her. That she couldn't possibly, because he'd never been able to. But he knew Jessie would hate that, so instead, he asked, "Do you want to talk about it?"

"No. Just leave me alone, Lattimer, okay?"

"Okay," he said, holding his palms out as if to ward off any angry words. "We won't talk. But I'm not leaving you alone. Not right now."

Jessie shrugged and disappeared into the tack room, a portion of her heart glad that he was nearby, sharing her pain in a small way.

"If you'd go out to dinner with me it might help to get your mind off things," Bodie suggested. He sat on the tack box watching Jessie scrub out an extra feed tub that really didn't need washing. Dan, Francine and Cissy had been gone for no more than ten minutes, and he had kept his promise. He hadn't spoken since the threesome had left. Not until now.

She flicked him a disgruntled glance and blew a wisp of hair from her eyes. "As you can no doubt tell, Mr. Lattimer, I have problems in my life. I sure don't want to add to them by going out with you, especially after you made such a big deal about starting over, then ignored me for three days."

"Missed me, have you?" he asked with a slow grin.

"About as much as you miss a case of the flu," she said with unmistakable sarcasm.

"Liar," he said cockily, in an attempt to change the direction of her thoughts. He knew Jessie. If he could get her riled up, she'd forget her problems with Cissy—at least for a while. "There's nothing to worry about, sweetheart. I've just been busy catching up on things, rounding up some clients."

Straightening, Jessie planted her hands on her hips, fully aware of what he was doing, yet still unable to stop herself from responding to him. She forced herself to remember the upsetting scene with her mother and the accusing look on Dan's face when he'd seen Bodie standing so close to her only moments before. Her face was bland and controlled as she asked, "Did anyone ever tell you you're conceited?"

A smile tugged at his lips. "Once or twice."

Jessie made a noise that sounded suspiciously like a snort. Actually, Bodie accepted his looks with an enviable casualness, considering those looks were the sort that made feminine heartbeats accelerate. "Don't you have work to do?'' she asked, trying to ignore her own pounding heart.

"Not really." He indicated his shirt. "I finished for the day and thought I'd come to do some courting."

"Oh. Is that what you call sitting around and watching me work?"

He shrugged. "Whatever."

"Look, why don't you go find something else to entertain you?" she pleaded, doing her best to ignore the fact that she was glad he was with her.

"I find you very entertaining, thank you. And if you'd let me, I'd help you."

"Thanks, but no thanks. Why don't you go talk to your dad?" she suggested, hope glowing in her dark eyes. She needed some breathing space, some time to get herself back together. He had the most uncanny way of rendering her completely thoughtless.

"He's at the racing secretary's office. Said he wanted to harass Phil's secretary about the male strip show."

Jessie's eyes widened. "Male strip show? She went to see the male strippers?"

"Yeah," he drawled with a wicked smile.

"I can't believe it!"

"Why? Wouldn't you like to go?"

"No!"

His eyebrows lifted in speculation and patent disbelief.

Jessie bent to her scrubbing once more and offered smugly, "If you've seen one naked man, you've seen them all." Even as she said it, she knew she was lying. She sneaked a peek at him from behind the veil of her lashes. The smile hovering around his mouth told her he knew she was lying.

"Naked women are different," he offered laconically.

"Bodie," she said, "can't we talk about something else?"

"Sure," he said agreeably. "Why won't you go out with me?"

"Not that."

"Then what?"

"What about your mother?" she asked almost desperately. "How is she? I haven't seen her in ages."

He leaned back against the wall, folding his arms across his chest and crossing his ankles indolently. "She's still as ornery as ever. Still trying to marry me off."

Jessie wiped a trickle of perspiration from her eyes with the back of her wrist. "Did you tell her it was a lost cause?" The tone of her voice held an astringent sweetness.

All the laughter fled his face. His green eyes were serious as he said, "Nope. I told her I was working on it."

Jessie's smile evaporated. How had he managed to do it to her again? Without warning, he'd once more taken their conversation from the mundane to the personal. She felt like crying again, but she'd die before she let him know it.

Scrubbing the already spotless feed tub with unnecessary force, she favored him with a withering look. "If you're talking about me, then you must have your mother's penchant for lost causes. I've had my share of bad relationships; I'm not interested in another."

"What you need, Jessie, is a man who appreciates you for what you are."

In a voice thick with contempt, she asked, "And I suppose you think you're that man?"

"I don't think it; I know it."

His confidence in himself was too much, especially when hers was so low. She didn't need him in her life now. Didn't want him... Ah, there was the real kicker. She'd never stopped wanting him. And it didn't help knowing that every time he came near her that fact was reinforced. All it did was bring back feelings of guilt because she'd married Dan when she still loved Bodie; so naturally, she didn't want Bodie around to remind her. Rising, she threw the scrub brush at the pail. Soapy water splashed up over her jean-clad legs and elicited a mild oath from her trembling lips.

"You conceited bastard!" she said, planting her wet fists on her hips and walking to within a foot of him. "Who do you think you are, coming back here and feeding me this line of bull after leaving me alone for six years?"

Bodie straightened. He'd watched the pain turn to anger, but he wasn't ready to be her scapegoat again. "Isn't that what you wanted me to do—leave you alone?" he offered with a logic she found totally unacceptable.

"You bet it was!" she snapped. "It's what I still want. You say you want to try again, but you'd better face facts, Lattimer! I'm just not the marrying kind— and I've got the divorce papers to prove it."

For the first time since they'd embarked on the rapidly deteriorating conversation, Jessie saw a hint of anger in his eyes at the mention of her divorce. He pushed himself to his feet, his six-foot four-inch frame dwarfing her. A trickle of apprehension slid down her spine. Why had mention of her divorce made him so angry?

"I'm really not interested in your divorce, Jessie, but I'd sure like to hear the reason you decided to marry someone else after you swore you loved me but turned my offer down flat."

The anger on her face disappeared with startling abruptness when confronted with his. She began to tremble. It wasn't fear of him and his fury that unnerved her, but the fact that he'd brought up the subject she'd just been thinking of—a subject she couldn't come to terms with. Still, there was no way she was going to admit her mistake to him.

He grasped her upper arm. "Tell, me, Jessie!" he snarled in a soft, accusing voice. "Tell me again how much you loved me, but couldn't marry me because marriage would interfere with your career. Then explain why you conveniently forgot all that when Dan Givens came along."

By the time he finished, the anguish in his voice had pushed aside the anger, but Jessie didn't realize it because it was the same anguish that was filling her own heart. She couldn't tell him anything he wanted to know because she didn't have any explanation. Not one that was acceptable, anyway. There was nothing she could do to change things. Nothing she could say to make things right. No way to make six long years of sorrow and hurt go away. All she could do was make certain it didn't happen again.

She knew Bodie as well as he knew her. She knew that until she made it very clear that she wasn't interested, he would keep trying to get her to come back to him. And every time he touched her, it was a little harder to stick by her convictions. She had to end their misery once and for all. They'd both suffered enough.

She jerked her arm free. "I don't owe you an explanation or anything else, Lattimer."

"Jessie . . ." His tone of voice was threatening.

She lifted her chin to look him straight in the eye and forced a venom she was far from feeling into her voice. "Go to hell!"

Before she could do more than register the shock of his face, she whirled and marched down the shedrow, headed anywhere that was away from him. She had taken no more than half a dozen steps when he grasped the soft flesh of her upper arm in a hard, hurting grip and hauled her around.

In a voice that sounded all the more menacing in its utter normalcy, he said, "I've been to hell, sweetheart. You sent me there. And the next time I go, I'm taking you with me."

Sleep, Jessie, sleep. The words, repeated innumerable times since she'd told Bodie to go to hell a week ago, bounced off her tired mind and were lost in the continuing maelstrom of her thoughts. Sleep was almost a thing of the past since he'd come back into her life. She punched the pillow and rolled onto her stomach.

Don't think about it, Jessie. But the scenario played out its various themes at will in her tired mind. She'd told him to go to hell, but instead, that's where she'd been. There was no way of knowing what he was feeling. She hadn't seen him since he'd released his bruising grip on her arm and walked away, leaving her standing desolately in the shedrow with her life in tatters at her feet for the second time. And it was all her own doing . . . again.

The only good to come of it was that she'd realized that her problems with her relationships were just that—her problems. She was the one at fault.

Jessie sighed deeply, a soft suspiration that sounded loud in the darkness. Why worry about it? She had no intention of getting involved with Bodie again. She'd been right to refuse his offer of marriage before, even if that had mostly been Vera's doing. Her marriage to Dan had taught her that she just wasn't cut out for the wedded state.

Her marriage. As usual when she thought of it, she was assailed with guilt for going so willfully into something she'd known deep within herself wasn't right. It was that recurring sense of guilt that prompted her outburst to Bodie that afternoon. What could she say? How could she tell him she'd still been in love with him when she'd married Dan? That by setting out to snare Dan Givens she'd only been trying to recapture the emotions and the sense of self-worth he, Bodie, had made her feel? How could she tell him that Dan's stable, respectable background had beckoned to her with the illusive promise of adding that respectability and permanence to her often looked down upon, nomadic life-style. Something marriage to another racetracker didn't offer.

Bodie. She rolled onto her side and wondered where he was and what he was doing. She'd heard he'd flown to California. Had he asked someone else out after her refusal? That thought sent her flopping onto her back once more. Did he sleep nights? Or was he lying awake wondering what had prompted him to say the things he had...as she was?

Chapter Four

Tap, tap, tap. Tap, tap, tap. The insistent rapping brought Jessie's lashes reluctantly upward. She stretched and rolled to her side, reasoning that if something had awakened her, she must have finally dozed off.

Tap, tap. Someone was knocking at the patio door. She pushed herself onto one elbow, darting a quick glance at the clock. Fifteen minutes before two. Her heart began to race. If someone was knocking at her door in the middle of the night, something must be wrong.

Swinging her feet to the side of the bed, Jessie groped her way down the hallway to the living room, not bothering to put a robe on over the Mickey Mouse T-shirt she often wore to bed. When she reached the kitchen, she flipped on the light and pushed aside the lightweight ivory-tinted drape covering the glass door.

A man's battered face was pressed against the surface of the glass, his nose flattened, his eyelids drooping over bloodshot eyes. A shriek escaped Jessie and she let go of the curtain to block out the sight, her hand moving up to cover the pulse that beat in her throat. With a pounding heart and a dry throat, she began to back away toward the phone.

"Jess . . ."

The voice coming from the other side of the door halted her retreat and drew her brows together.

"Open the door, Jessie."

Bodie. The breath she'd been holding whooshed from her and she moved toward the door on shaking legs. Just to make sure, she pushed the curtain aside once more. It was Bodie, all right, but her relief was mingled with disgust. He was three sheets to the wind, and he'd been fighting. He stood looking at her, dressed in freshly starched Wranglers and a wrinkled shirt, his face still smashed against the glass, a silly grin and a fair amount of blood on his face. She dropped the curtain and, unlocking the door, tried to push it open, an impossible task since he was leaning on it.

"Stand up, Bodie!"

"Can't," came the cheerful reply.

"Great!" Jessie muttered. "Lean against the door-jamb," she commanded.

Raking the fabric aside, she watched as he shifted his weight to the side, then she swooshed the door open and he more or less fell into the room—and straight into her waiting arms. She grabbed him around his waist and took his weight with a soft "Ugh!" He was heavy and smelled of beer and perfume. Anger replaced her disgust. "What are you doing here?"

"I came t' talk."

"You're drunk, Bodie."

"I'm not drunk. I'm feeling good," he corrected.

"And from the looks of your face, you can't be feeling too good—or thinking too straight," she continued, as if he hadn't corrected her on the degree of his sobriety...or drunkenness. "How about coming back tomorrow?"

"No, Jess. I need to see you...to talk...t'night." He punched the air with a decisive forefinger.

"All right," she agreed with a sigh of reluctance, "but stand up, will you?"

His head snapped back and he put his hands on her hips to steady himself. His caressing hand moved lower on her hip as, weaving, he grinned down at her and slurred conversationally, "Did I wake you up?"

Jessie closed her eyes and clenched her teeth together, praying for patience. She dug her nails into his hand and moved it higher. Then, lifting her lashes to glare up at him, she said, "Heavens, no. I was working on my cross-stitch."

"Really?" he asked. "C'n I see?"

She rolled her eyes. "I was being sarcastic, Bodie. It's two o'clock in the morning. Of course you woke me up!"

The smile on his face vanished in an instant. He tried to stand alone, swayed and dropped his hands to her shoulders. "Oh. Then I guess you're purty mad, huh?"

Jessie looked at him. His face looked as if he'd taken on Sugar Ray Leonard, he smelled like a Milwaukee brewery—or a perfume lab—but nevertheless, he was there, with her.

Smiling a silly smile, he reached out and brushed her cheek with one finger. She pushed his hand away. She didn't want to feel his touch, but the truth was, she was afraid of what that touch might do to her new resolve. Sober or drunk, serious or acting the fool as she remembered he could do when the situation warranted, Bodie Lattimer was hard to resist.

She begrudged the smile curving her lips. "Yeah," she said, with a nod of her head. "I'm pretty mad."

"Both of you?" he asked seriously.

"Both of me?"

"Yeah." He held up two fingers. "I can see two of you."

Jessie groaned. "You aren't going to be sick, are you?"

The affronted look on his face was comical. "Sick? Of course I'm not going to be sick. I can hold my beer," he told her with as much dignity as he could muster under the circumstances.

"Sure, you can," she soothed, attempting to head him toward the sofa.

Bodie's arm hung across her shoulders as, leaning against her, he stumbled across the room. When his fingers—accidentally or otherwise—brushed against her breast, she drew in a sharp breath, her gaze flying to his.

"Oops!" he apologized, with a gleam in his eyes that negated the apology. Definitely *otherwise* she thought grimly, releasing him so that he fell onto the fat, floral cushions.

"Stay put," she told him crisply. "Let me get something for your face."

"I'll be the one right here," he promised, easing his head back.

Jessie threw him a fulminating look, which was wasted because his eyes were closed.

She returned in a matter of moments, armed with a bowl of warm water, a cloth and some antiseptic, which she set on the overturned half of a whiskey barrel that doubled as a coffee table. Easing to the edge of the sofa beside him, she commanded, "Sit up."

One eye—the one that wasn't beginning to swell— opened and glared up at her with reproach. Seeing the uncompromising look in hers, he levered himself upward and propped himself against the pillows piled in the sofa's corner.

Jessie wrung the water from the cloth and held it out to him. "Here. You do your nose."

Taking the washcloth, he held the soothing warmth to his aching flesh a moment before attempting to clean the blood away. When he finished, he handed the cloth back to Jessie, who washed it clean and then began to dab at the cut above his eye. A muscle twitching in his jaw was the only movement he made.

Bodie didn't want to move, didn't want to do anything but sit there with his eyes closed and breathe in the clean, fresh and feminine soap smell that emanated from Jessie's sleep-warm body. He let his lashes drift open. She wore a look that, even in his rapidly sobering state, he recognized as the one she wore when she was saddling a horse in the paddock. Intense. Determined. Caring.

He watched as she turned away to rinse the cloth. When she faced him again, with the cloth aimed for the corner of his mouth, their glances collided. Her hand stopped in midair. Awareness palpitated between them. The resolve to keep him out of her life withered by slow degrees as feelings she'd hoped were dead and buried struggled to breathe new life.

"Jessie..." The plea in his voice broke the spell of longing gripping her, and her trembling hand continued toward its destination with renewed determination.

"Be still," she commanded, reminding herself somewhat desperately that nothing had changed. She dabbed at the cut, her movements less gentle than before.

"Ouch!" Bodie protested with a frown, grabbing her wrist. "What's the matter with you?"

Her eyes widened in feigned innocence. "Nothing."

"Then take it easy, huh?"

Exasperated with him, herself and the whole situation, Jessie dropped the cloth into the bowl and rose. "I'll get you a pillow and you can sleep this off," she said.

He stared up at her with smoldering eyes that gradually lost their antagonism. "I don't wanna sleep. I told you, I want...need to talk to you, Jess. Please."

Jessie felt her resolve melting beneath the urgency radiating from him. She nodded. "All right. How about some coffee, then?"

"Fine. Good." He levered himself up. "Where's the bathroom?"

"Bodie..."

"I'm not gonna be sick," he said with a wave of his hand.

"Down the hall."

Pushing himself to his feet, he headed down the hallway. Halfway there he turned and said, "You make the coffee. I'll be back in a shake."

Jessie was measuring the coffee grinds into a paper filter when she heard the shower running. She sighed and hoped he didn't flood the place.

Moments later, she heard his deep bass voice singing a drunken rendition of Don Henley's "You Must Not Be Drinking Enough." Her heart ached curiously when he sang about selling what was left of his soul for another round with the unnamed woman, a woman who got a name—Jessie—in a later verse, which told how she had stepped on his pride and passed on his passion. Jessie stood in the center of the kitchen listening, wondering if she was the reason he'd set out to get drunk, and hurting for all the pain they'd both suffered.

The coffee had finished dripping before Bodie found his way back to the living area, clad in nothing but his jeans and carrying his boots and shirt. Jessie, her defenses lowered considerably by the message of the tear-jerking song, tried to ignore the mesmerizing pull of his naked chest. Tried to forget how many times she'd pressed kisses to the coppery nipples hiding in the swirling cloud of black hair, and how many times her caressing fingertips had followed the fine line of hair that disappeared into the low-riding waist-band of his jeans.

Instead, she forced herself to acknowledge that he was walking much better and that his eyes, though bloodshot, looked as if he'd sobered up some. His hair was wet, and he'd combed it straight back. The severity of the style accentuated the masculine bone structure of his face and made the ravages of his fight more pronounced.

"Why were you fighting?" The words sounded loud in the stillness. She hadn't meant to ask. Hadn't meant for him to know she was concerned.

Bodie's eyes, filled with something akin to embarrassment, met hers then slid away. "It doesn't matter."

He even sounded more sober, she thought, pouring them both coffee. She carried it to the sofa, leaned over and set it on the coffee table. Her face was near his—so close she could smell the clean scent of her mouthwash he'd used. She could see the flecks of brown in his eyes and count the fine lines that radiated from their corners. His eyes mirrored her own features, and the longing and indecision on her face. Seeing the indecision stiffened Jessie's resolve. Straightening with lightning abruptness, she forced herself to remember why he was there.

"What did you want to talk about?"

Bodie reflected on his own conflicting emotions. How could he tell her that he had come to her not because he wanted to talk, but just because he wanted to see her? How could he tell her that he'd fought with Sloan Seavers because Sloan had insinuated in a nastily chauvinistic tone that Jessie couldn't train a horse?

And how could he tell her that the sight of her in her bikini panties and a T-shirt was driving him crazy with memories? Memories that made him want to loosen her hair from the confines of the single braid that hung over one shoulder and strip the clothes from her so that nothing, *nothing* was between them except the blazing passion they'd always shared.

"Talk?" he repeated.

Sighing in exasperation and sinking to the other end of the sofa, she reminded him, "You said you wanted to talk to me. What do you want to talk about?"

He picked up his coffee cup. "Oh, yeah. I wanted to talk about us."

"There is no 'us,' Bodie."

"There should have been," he told her, his countenance serious.

"Maybe," she conceded.

"There could be again."

Jessie shook her head. "No."

"Why?"

"Because nothing has changed, Bodie. I still have my dreams and ambitions. Dreams and ambitions that most men can't understand or accept. I've learned that the hard way."

His eyes narrowed. "You talkin' about Seavers?"

Surprise that he knew about her association with Sloan was evident on Jessie's face. "What do you know about Sloan?"

"I talked to Vera after I got back from California the other day."

"And she told you about Sloan?" Jessie asked, aghast.

Bodie took a sip of the hot coffee, burned his mouth and swore softly. "Yep. Everything."

He took another cautious slurp of the hot brew and looked at her again. "She said you didn't have any use for men these days because of Seavers. Is that true, Jess? Is that what all this has been about since I came back?"

Jessie knew she had to make him believe her . . . had to finish what she had started in the shedrow a week ago. Her heart was filled to the bursting point because severing—again—whatever it was that bound her to Bodie hurt so much.

Staring back at him with an intensity born of desperation, she said, "It's true. I won't take a back seat to anyone, Bodie, and I won't pander to any man's ego."

"You wouldn't have to with me, sweetheart," he said earnestly, his voice reflecting his rapidly sobering state. "I'm not like Seavers."

"Aren't you?"

"Hell no! Seavers loves the limelight and doesn't want to share it. Why else do you think he gave you the old heave-ho?"

Jessie's face paled at the heartless observation. Her mother had indeed told him everything.

Her shock and embarrassment wiped the last traces of drunkenness from Bodie's mind. Ashamed that he'd let his mouth run away with him again, he set his cup to the table and, resting his elbow on the arm of the sofa, leaned his forehead into his hand. "I'm sorry," he said at last.

When she didn't answer, he turned his head to look at her.

She sat leaning against one corner of the sofa, her bare legs tucked beneath her, the faded Mickey Mouse T-shirt covering the gentle swell of her breasts, which rose and fell with every breath she took. Her eyes were bright with pain, pain he had inflicted.

Wanting to make amends, he said, "Michelle Du Pree is perfect for Seavers."

When the hurt in her eyes only intensified, he swore and reached for his coffee cup again, downing half its contents regardless of the heat. *Think before you speak, Lattimer.*

"What I mean," he began in an attempt to cover his error, "is Seavers knows you're a better horseman than he is. He wasn't about to stick around so you could show him up—something that will never happen with Michelle, since her IQ rivals that of a turnip."

Jessie continued to stare at a spot across the room, trying to digest this new information.

"He wasn't right for you, Jess."

Unable to accept that the problem with her relationship with Sloan was his fault instead of hers, she said, "He's a top trainer, he's handsome—"

"He's a bloodsucker who bleeds his clients for every drop of money he can get!" Bodie cut in. "He couldn't train his way out of a paper bag!"

"Then how do you explain his standing as third leading trainer?"

"Aw, c'mon, Jess. I could be third leading trainer, too, if someone would buy me the kind of horses he has." He paused, trying to gauge her feelings. Finally, he said, "What you need, Jessie, is someone who appreciates you for what you are. You're a lot of woman; you need a lot of man."

"And you think you're that man?" she asked with thinly veiled sarcasm.

He shrugged, but she could see the affirmative answer in his eyes.

In spite of the varied emotions he'd subjected her to for the past half hour, Jessie stifled a wry inner smile. He hadn't changed. Six years had only tempered the cockiness and confidence in himself. No doubt about it, he was still as big a danger to her heart as he had been before. Maybe more. What they needed, she thought, was a different topic of conversation.

Rising, she moved closer to him and reached for his cup. Before she touched it, she felt the warmth of his hand as he reached to grasp the bend of her knee. Her eyes flew to his face and tingling tremors of pleasure shot through her.

"You know, Bodie," she said, in an attempt to camouflage the desire unfurling through her, "you and Sloan have one thing in common."

"What's that?" he said, smiling up at her while his hand began a leisurely upward journey.

"Your colossal egos!"

The momentary surprise on his face brought an uncontrollable giggle to Jessie's lips. The laughter transposed into a shriek when Bodie reached for her and flung her onto the sofa, pinning her there with one leg.

Denim chaffed her naked thighs as one bare foot rubbed over hers. His bare chest, smelling of feminine, flowery soap, pressed against her breast. One huge hand gripped her braided hair; the other held her wrist. As it always had, his unrelenting maleness made her acutely and uncomfortably aware of her own femininity. Speechless, she was able only to stare up at him with wide, waiting eyes.

"And you and I have something in common, too."

"What?" The question was the merest suspiration of sound.

"This." His head lowered; his hand moved from her hair to her breast.

Jessie damned the traitorous reaction of her flesh as her breast swelled to fill his palm. Their mouths were so close that nothing separated them but a heartbeat.

"No," she whispered.

He ignored the plea and their lips were actually touching when she whispered, "Please..."

Something in the tone of her voice stopped him. He drew back to look at her and was surprised to see the sheen of tears glittering in her eyes.

"Why?" he rumbled softly.

Her head moved from side to side. "I can't. Not now."

With his hand still covering her breast, he stared down at her, as if to discern what was written in her heart by the message in her eyes. Then he smiled, a funny, heartrending half-smile that lifted the heavy swathe of his mustache. He laced his fingers with hers, palm to palm, pulse to pulse. His thumb gently rubbed hers before he brought her hand to his mouth and pressed a kiss to each knuckle.

"Maybe you're right," he said, moved by her petition. "I'm pretty drunk." But even as he said it, she knew he was lying. He'd never been more sober than he was at the moment.

She nodded again. His fingers smoothed and stretched the soft knit of her T-shirt tautly over her aching breast. The pebble hardness of her nipple thrust against it, begging for attention, contrary to her words. It was attention Bodie promptly provided as he lowered his head and favored the soft flesh with a brief, passionless kiss.

It was all Jessie could do to keep from crying out in pleasure. As it was, her hands were just inches from his dark head before she came to her senses enough to realize that any weakening in her shaky defenses would lead to a total defeat. Instead, she put her hands on his shoulders and gave him a halfhearted push.

Bodie took the hint and sat up, turning his back to her. With his elbows resting on his knees and the heels of his hands pressed against his eyes, he was the picture of abject misery. In spite of her good intentions, Jessie couldn't stop the hand that reached out and touched his bare, tanned skin.

The action froze him so that she couldn't even feel him breathing. But gradually his tense muscles relaxed beneath her touch and he lowered his hands to dangle between his thighs. Glancing over his shoulder at her, he said, "I'm whipped. Can I have that pillow now?"

Jessie knew what was happening. He was taking things back to the normal. Back to the unimportant, the mundane. There was too much between them. Too many unspoken questions, too many explanations and too many inadequate answers to tackle at the moment. The best thing to do was to get out of the current volatile situation with as little pain as possible.

"I'll get it."

Smiling a weak thanks, he moved so that she could get up and his brooding gaze burned into her back as she disappeared down the hallway. When she returned, she carried a geometric-patterned sheet and a pillow in a matching case. He took them from her with a brief "Thanks."

"I'll try not to wake you when I leave in the morning," she told him.

"Don't worry about it."

"I'll leave the coffeepot plugged in."

"Good. I'll probably need it."

Jessie matched his dry smile and twisted her fingers together. "Well . . . good night."

"Good night."

She started toward her bedroom, then turned. "If you need anything, call."

"I will," he promised.

She headed toward her room again.

"Jessie . . ."

She spun around quickly. "Yes?"

"Dream about me."

Speechless, breathless, she could only stare at him before she turned and fled to the sanctuary of her room.

The sound of the door closing roused Bodie from a confusing dream. Jessie was leaving, he thought, opening his eyes and turning on his side. His head protested the sudden movement and his body screamed with agony at being forced to rest on a sofa that was at least a foot and a half too short. With a groan, he pushed himself to a sitting position, seriously contemplating sabotage of all the breweries in Milwaukee.

Still wearing his jeans, he got to his feet and headed for the bathroom and, he hoped, some aspirin. Two minutes later he gave up the search and opted to go back to bed. Eyeing the sofa with a jaded gaze, he grabbed his boots and shirt and ambled to Jessie's room. Though fairly small, it was cheerfully and femininely decorated in peach and pale blue, even down to the eyelet-trimmed sheets on the bed.

He sank onto the bed's softness, a sigh of relief soughing from his lips. The clean, fresh scent he associated with Jessie surrounded him, drugging his senses and filling his aching head with sweet memories. Reaching for the extra pillow, he turned onto his side and buried his face in it, imagining, in his mind, that it was Jessie's hair. Then, breathing in the sunshiny fragrance of her shampoo, he drifted into a healing sleep.

It had been a heck of a day, Jessie thought when she unlocked the trailer door and went inside, hot, tired and longing for a shower. On top of a heck of a night. She glanced at the sofa and saw with a sinking heart that Bodie was gone. The rumpled sheet and the pillow, which still bore the indentation where his head had lain, were the only testimony that the night had really happened. With a sigh, she gathered up the sheet, stripped off the pillowcase and threw them into the hamper.

What was she going to do with him? she asked herself as she straightened the living room. And what was she going to do with her own runaway feelings? Why was it that every time he came around, her goals and plans for the future dissolved beneath his smile and the melting heat of his eyes? What was it about him that swept away the remembrances of her other failed relationships and made her long to try again with him?

She didn't know. She only knew that she didn't like the seesawing of her emotions and the fluctuating degrees of her resolve not to make another mistake.

Wiping it all from her mind, she went into the bathroom, pulled off her clothes and stepped into the shower, letting its cool spray soothe away the heat of the day and the weariness left by her sleeplessness after she'd left Bodie on the sofa. She only wished she could wash away the memories of Bodie as easily. But she couldn't, and they swirled around inside her head in spite of her wishes to the contrary... Bodie smiling that naughty, lecherous smile when his hand had brushed her breast. Bodie telling her seriously that he could hold his beer. Bodie looking down at her with an emotion in his eyes that she didn't want to acknowledge...

Stepping from the shower, she bundled her wet hair in a towel and dried her damp body with another. She was picking up her dirty clothes when something white caught her eye. She shook her head in disbelief. Bodie's underwear. Wondering how she would get it back to him, she tossed it into the dirty-clothes hamper at the same time as she heard someone knocking.

She pulled on the hip-length terry robe hanging on the back of the bathroom door and hurried to answer the knock. Opening the door, she was surprised to see Francine and Cissy standing there. Somehow, she had expected Dan to bring Cissy home.

Dressed with a casual flair that shouted money, Jessie's former husband's new wife wore her wealth and her happiness well. Cissy wore a new shorts set and a chocolate smile.

"Hi, Mom!" she cried, launching herself at Jessie's bare legs.

"Hi, sugar," Jessie answered, smoothing the child's hair while her eyes questioned Francine.

"Hello," Francine said, brushing back her sleek tobacco-brown hair. "Here she is. All safe and sound, if a bit gooey."

Forcing an answering smile to her lips and breathing a prayer of thanks that she'd straightened up the living room, Jessie said, "So I see. Where's Dan?"

"He had a meeting this morning, so I told him I'd bring Cissy home," Francine explained. She eyed Jessie's state of undress, an apology in her blue eyes. "I'm sorry if we caught you at a bad time."

"That's okay," Jessie assured her, trying as hard as Francine was to make the situation as pleasant as possible. "I just got in from the track and took a quick shower. Come on in."

Cissy burst into the living room and Jessie helped Francine with the child's belongings, which seemed to have doubled since she'd been gone.

"I'm afraid we've spoiled her," the dark-haired woman admitted, placing a brand-new stuffed animal on top of a table near the door.

Great! "No problem," Jessie assured her with a half-smile. "Sometimes, I'm afraid I don't spoil her enough. It'll probably even out just right."

"I hope so."

Longing for nothing more than an end to the situation, Jessie nevertheless urged her manners forward. "Would you like a glass of tea, or I can make some fresh coffee?"

"Oh, no, thanks. I'm supposed to stop by my mother's for lunch," Francine declined. "But I would like to get this chocolate off my hands, if you don't mind."

"Of course not," Jessie said, hoping her relief didn't show. She breathed a prayer of thankfulness that the bathroom was spotless and that she'd found and disposed of Bodie's underwear. "The bathroom is just down the hall on the left."

"Thanks."

While Francine washed away the candy, Cissy announced proudly, "I did some chores for Francine and she gave me a 'lowance. I bought you a present, Mom."

"Really, sugar?" Jessie said, her heart constricting at the caring Cissy showed for her. She watched the child digging through the contents of a shopping bag, a look of concentration molding her small features.

"Here it is!" Cissy announced at last, holding up a ceramic mouse to add to Jessie's collection of miniatures.

"Oh, Cissy, it's beautiful," Jessie told her, examining the gift closely. "Just look at his little ears!"

"She picked it out all by herself," Francine said, entering the room.

Jessie looked up from the mouse and met the other woman's eyes. Was it possible that she saw a tentative overture of friendliness there? Was it possible that Francine wasn't her enemy after all?

"Cissy, why don't you take this into my bedroom and put it on the shelf," she suggested, wanting to thank Francine in private.

"Okay!" Cissy chorused, heading for Jessie's room and singing a popular country song.

"I appreciate you teaching her about chores and the value of money," Jessie said, offering a tentative olive branch.

"Thank you for bringing up a really wonderful little girl," Francine returned. Then, as if she were aware that the compliment embarrassed Jessie, she said, "Well, I'd better be go..." Her voice trailed away and a frown filled her face as she looked past Jessie and asked, "Cissy? What's the matter?"

Startled by the unexpected interruption, Jessie turned to see what was wrong.

Cissy stood near the bar that separated the kitchen from the living room, her eyes wide and questioning.

"What is it, Cissy?" Jessie asked, her frown matching Francine's.

"Mom?" Cissy questioned. "What's Mr. Bodie doin' in your bed?"

The innocent query sent Francine's gaze flying from Cissy to Jessie, shock drawing a gasp from her lips.

That same shock drew all the blood from Jessie's face and froze her to immobility. Bodie in her bed? He *couldn't* be, could he? But the look on Cissy's face vouched for her words. Five-year-olds didn't lie about such things. And the look on Francine's face told her that she knew it.

Chapter Five

"Well, I really should be going," Francine said nervously, breaking the silence that seemed to border on eternity.

The words jolted Jessie from her stupor, and she leaped to her feet. "Uh, there really is a simple explanation for this."

Francine held up her hand, palm outward. "Please. You don't owe me any explanation."

Needing to tell Francine what happened and wanting to throw Bodie's thoughtlessness back in his face, Jessie turned to Cissy and said, "Go keep Bodie company for a moment, sugar. He'll tell you what he was doing in my bed."

"Okay, Mom."

When the child had gone, Jessie regarded Francine, who was twisting the strap of her leather purse.

"You've already got your mind made up about what happened here last night, don't you, Francine? You think I took advantage of the fact that Cissy was with you and spent the night with Bodie Lattimer."

Francine couldn't quite meet her eyes. "It's really none of my concern."

"I came here stinking drunk."

The masculine voice brought Francine's head up and sent Jessie whirling toward its sound. Fully dressed, Bodie stood in the kitchen, Cissy in his arms and a look of severe contrition on his face. "Jessie let me sleep on the sofa. When she got up and went to work this morning, I got up and went to her bed to finish sleeping it off. She didn't even know I was still here."

Francine didn't say anything, and her guarded expression defied reading. He turned his attention to Jessie. "I'm sorry, Jess. I never meant for anything like this to happen."

But it did. She wanted to tell him that his presence had jeopardized her already rocky relationship with Dan. She wanted to scream at him, to tell him to get out of her life and leave her alone. But how could she when the look in his eyes spoke of a sorrow too deep to put into words, and her daughter—the tiny bone of contention between her and her ex-husband—twined her arms around Bodie's neck and rested her cheek against his whisker-stubbled one in total acceptance.

The anger in Jessie fizzled out as quickly as it had kindled, leaving behind the bitter ashes of regret and an aching, soul-deep weariness.

"Well, I really do need to go," Francine said at last, heading for the door. "Cissy, I'll pick you up on Friday morning, okay?"

Entranced by the froth of dark hair that peeked from the vee of Bodie's shirt, the child only nodded.

"Well . . . goodbye."

"Goodbye." Jessie's voice was almost nonexistent. She watched the other woman leave with a feeling of foreboding in her heart. Would she tell Dan? Probably. Her heart sank. The possible repercussions were astronomical.

"Are you all right?" Bodie's voice brought her eyes to his.

Looking at him with a countenance devoid of feeling, she said in a neutral voice, "Sure. I'm fine."

"You look like hell."

Her lips kicked up at the corners in a small, sarcastic smile. "Thanks. I wonder why?"

"Are you mad at Bodie?" Cissy, in tune with the tension in the room, piped up.

Jessie's head moved in a negative motion. "No."

"I'm messing up your life, huh?"

Crossing her arms tightly in front of her to keep herself from flying into a million irreparable pieces, she nodded. "You could say that."

"And I need to stay away?"

"Yes," she whispered.

This time it was Bodie's head that moved up and down. She watched as he transferred his attention to the child in his arms, whispering something that was inaudible from Jessie's place across the room. Then, without another word, he lowered Cissy to the floor and started for the door. When he reached it, he

turned, a look on his face that was something between determination and sorrow.

"I'll try. But I can't make any promises."

The door closed behind him. Jessie watched him go,
the same feelings at war in her heart.

Bodie walked out of the trailer and moved swiftly
down the street and out of Jessie's life. His long strides
gobbled up the asphalt as he headed toward the en-
trance of the trailer park and a pay phone so he could
call someone to come and pick him up. He'd left his
truck at the bar situated on the once-infamous but
now fading Bossier Strip, and had presumed on a
stranger to drive him to Jessie's.

Why, he asked as the sun beat mercilessly down on
his aching head and caused his stomach to churn, did
she refuse to give him the same chance she'd allowed
Givens and Seavers? Didn't she care enough? The
thought sent his despair plummeting to new levels.

Jessie. A picture of her face when he'd left and the
memory of all the misery he'd brought to her just by
wanting to be with her the night before was enough to
make anyone swear off drinking. And, while besting
Seavers in the fight had given him a momentary sense
of accomplishment, it still didn't solve the problem
with Dan. He forced one foot in front of the other. He
couldn't fight the whole world for her. He wondered
what it would take to make her see how easy the so-
lution to her problems could be. How easy the solu-
tion had always been.

Bodie was almost to the clubhouse when the sound
of an approaching vehicle brought his head up. He
swore when he recognized the familiar truck. Just

when he'd thought his day couldn't possibly get any worse, here came Vera. Hoping she would pass on by, he didn't even slow his steps. His hope died a sudden death when she braked to a halt beside him.

Urging a cocky grin to his lips, he made his eyes meet hers. The smile slipped a bit when he failed to encounter the rancor he usually saw there. The look in her dark eyes was as close to approval as he was ever likely to see. Wondering what he'd done to deserve it, he drawled, "Mornin', Vera. Or is it noon by now?"

"Just past," she said. "Been to Jessie's?"

Why lie, Lattimer? She isn't stupid.

"Yeah. I spent the night there," he confessed, opting for the truth. His tone asked her without words what she planned to do about it.

"That figures," Vera said, confident that since he'd been drunk and fighting Jessie wouldn't have let anything happen between them. "Where are you going? I'll drop you off."

Bodie couldn't hide the surprise in his eyes. "The track."

"Hop in."

A slow smile curved his lips. "You aren't going to knock me off and dump me in Bistineau, are you?"

Vera matched his smile with one of her own. "I've thought about it. Someone probably should, but not this time. I owe you one."

His surprise deepened. "You do?"

"Yeah." The smile seeped into her eyes. "You whipped Seavers, didn't you?"

He nodded.

"Why?"

"Because of something he said about Jessie."

"That figures, too," Vera said with a nod. "Hop in."

Still uncomprehending, but reasoning that he'd come out a notch above in some sort of mental score-card Vera kept, Bodie rounded the hood of the truck and opened the door. He slid onto the seat, drawing in a deep breath of the welcome coolness. He glanced at Vera as she put the truck into drive. "Thanks."

"Don't mention it."

Another week passed. A long, agonizing week in which Bodie did what he said he would try to do. He stayed away. He went to South Louisiana to work for a few days. It was a week that was emotionally and psychologically debilitating as the backside buzzed with speculation about Jessie and Bodie and why he had fought Sloan Seavers. It was a week Jessie spent worrying and wondering whether or not Francine would say anything to Dan about Cissy's startling discovery. By the following Friday, it appeared that she hadn't, and when Francine picked Cissy up for the weekend, the conversation danced around the subject, just as their eyes danced away from each other every time their glances met.

Francine drove off with Cissy in the front seat of her new Mercedes, and Jessie went inside her ten-year-old remodeled trailer, feeling that her whole life was out of control and careening toward a terrible disaster.

She was watching television later that night and eating a frozen pizza when the phone rang. Transferring the pizza slice to her left hand, she picked up the receiver. "Hello."

"Is Lattimer there?" Dan's voice, full of fury, greeted her salutation.

Jessie's heart sank. *You did it after all, Francine.* She put the partially eaten slice of pizza on the plate and sat up straighter, preparing for whatever Dan had to say. "No."

"Good. I wouldn't want your lover to hear this," he told her in a voice that would have made the Arctic seem warm.

Blood roared in her ears and she felt as if she might faint for the first time in her life. Her mouth moved stiffly, her lips forming the words he had to believe. "Bodie isn't my lover."

"No? Cissy told me he was in your bed the other day."

So, the traitor hadn't been Francine, but Cissy, who, with a child's innocence, had let it slip. "He isn't my lover," she reiterated.

"If you really think I believe that . . ."

The sullen disbelief in his voice hurt. After all, they had been married once, and even though it hadn't worked out, she had never done anything to deserve this opinion of her. Stung more than she wanted to admit, she said, "It's the truth!"

"Tell it to the judge!" Dan snarled.

What bit of color still in Jessie's face faded, leaving her deathly pale. She pressed her palm against her forehead, trying to stop the whirling mélange of words. Her voice was the merest thread of sound. "What?"

"You heard me. I'm suing for full custody of Celeste. She doesn't need to be around a mother who sleeps around."

"I don't sleep around!"

"Celeste needs a mother who will be with her. Someone who will do things with her, take proper care of her."

Unexpected anger meshed with Jessie's fear. It was one thing for Dan to question her morality, another for him to insinuate that she didn't take proper care of Cissy. Jessie's voice found a note of conviction. "I do take proper care of her! You have no right to suggest—"

"No, I don't have many rights now, but you can rest assured that will change as soon as is legally possible."

Her knuckles turned white as she gripped the receiver. Pain, fury and terror all fought for supremacy of her heart. "You bring my baby home Sunday evening, like you're supposed to!"

"Oh, I will," Dan said with smooth confidence. "But it will be the last time."

Then there was nothing but a buzzing in her ear. Dan had hung up. Jessie replaced the phone and sat staring at it in disbelief. Her eyes drifted shut and she leaned back against the sofa.

It was just a bad dream. Dan hadn't really called and said what he'd said.

As soon as is legally possible.

Tears started in her eyes and slid down her cheeks. Only when she tasted their saltiness did she realize that the scene had really happened. It wasn't a dream. Dan really had jerked her life out from under her. And with a carelessness that was appalling.

The phone rang again, bringing her back to reality and drying her tears. What if it were Dan calling back?

It rang a third time, but she didn't answer it. Mute, fearful, she sat and counted the rings until it stopped. Then she collapsed onto the sofa and let the tidal wave of sorrow wash over her and tow her under.

She wasn't certain how long she lay with a pounding head and arid, aching eyes, trying to make some sense out of the turmoil raging inside her head, but it seemed only a matter of minutes until she heard banging on the door. Her head lifted in response to the noise and she considered the possibilities. Dan? No. He'd accomplished what he'd set out to do for now. Then who? Vera. The thought that it was probably her mother brought a groan of dismay to her lips.

"Jessie! Are you all right?"

The sound of Bodie's voice made her bolt to a sitting position. Thank God! It didn't matter that he was indirectly the cause of her misery. Didn't matter that she'd told him to stay away. All that mattered was that in his arms was a peace and contentment she'd never found with anyone else. Jessie rose and crossed to the door on legs that trembled. Flinging it open, she stood looking up at the face that haunted her nights and her days, the face of the man she had never been able to forget—and probably never would.

Bodie couldn't miss the anguish reflected in her eyes or the ravages left on her face. She was always in control; he had never seen her look so crushed, so defeated. "Jessie...?"

His voice broke the silence yawning between them. With a small cry, she moved the two feet that separated them and, throwing her arms around his neck, pressed her face against his shoulder.

In an instinctive gesture, his arms closed around her and pulled her closer. Whatever had sent her into his arms, while obviously terrible, brought a prayer of thanks to his mind. He moved his hands over her back in a soothing, caring way, wanting to wipe away whatever was hurting her. Jessie responded by tightening her hold. Bodie's lashes drifted shut and his head tipped skyward, an I-can't-believe-this-but-thank-you-God look on his face that slowly changed to one of supreme peace as they stood in the gathering twilight shadows absorbing the very essence of one another.

Long, long moments later, he nuzzled her ear with his lips and said, "Are you all right?"

Pulling back to look at him with tormented eyes, she nodded.

"How about I come in, we have some coffee and you tell me what happened?"

Jessie offered him a hesitant smile and stepped aside. She fixed the coffee while Bodie stood leaning against the cabinets with his arms crossed, just watching her. Neither spoke until the coffeepot was switched on.

"What happened, Jess? Where's Cissy, and why didn't you answer the phone when I called a few minutes ago?"

She looked surprised. "Was that you?"

"Yeah." He attempted a smile that didn't quite materialize. "I was breaking the rules and calling you. I told you I couldn't promise to stay away."

He waited for her to say something about his transgression, but when she didn't, he continued, "I was worried sick when you didn't answer."

"Why? I might have just gone out somewhere."

"No. I knew you were here." A spasm of embarrassment crossed his features. "I'd already driven by and knew you were at home."

Instead of being angry, Jessie was touched by the fact that he had driven by to check on her. "Where did you call from?"

"The pay phone outside the park clubhouse."

He'd been so close. Without realizing that she did so, Jessie held out her hand, palm up, with her fingers curled inward. Without hesitation, Bodie placed his palm down, hooking his own curled fingers over hers, lifting her hand and meshing their fingers together. He pulled her nearer to where he stood.

His voice, always deep, seemed to tumble from his very soul as he commanded, "Tell me, Jessie."

Drawing in a fortifying breath, she said, "Dan called just before you did."

Understanding dawned slowly on Bodie's face. "And?"

"And...after a few insults, he told me that he's taking me to court to get custody of Cissy."

He swore softly, harshly. "It's because I was here, isn't it? Francine told him."

"It's because of you, but Cissy told him, not Francine."

"Cissy?"

"Yes. Most kids are innately honest and tell everything they know. She didn't know it would cause trouble." She turned their hands until Bodie's lay on top of hers. "I told him that we weren't having an affair. He didn't believe me."

"I'll go talk to him."

"No!" Jessie exhaled a tired sigh. "Just leave it alone. You don't know Dan. That would only make things worse."

"He can't get her, can he?"

She shrugged. "I don't know. I don't think so. I think they would have to prove that I'm unfit." She offered him a bitter smile. "I'm not perfect by a long shot, but I don't think I've done such a bad job with her."

"You've done a great job with her from what I've seen," he said truthfully. "She's warm, loving, mannerly..."

"Thanks," Jessie whispered, a lump forming in her throat. She squeezed his hand. "I'm glad you're here."

Bodie snorted in disbelief. "Glad? You oughtta kick me out for what I've done to you."

"You haven't done anything."

"I've screwed up your life."

Jessie's lips twisted into a wry smile. "I believe I've done that all by myself. And superbly, too, I might add."

Bodie turned their hands and brought hers to his lips. For some reason, he knew that the time was right to bring up the past. "Have you done what you set out to do, Jess?"

She knew what he was talking about. When she'd let him go, she'd vowed she'd be the top woman trainer in the country in ten years. Without warning, she was suddenly very aware of the length of his body so close to hers, and of the warmth emanating from his denim-sheathed thighs. "Have you been reading about me in the racing form?" she countered with a saucy smile that was designed to cover the yearning growing inside her.

"No."

"Then your question is answered."

"It's a tough business."

"It is that," she agreed. Looking at him with a question in her eyes, she said, "I don't understand it, Bodie. I know as much as any man out there."

"I know."

"Then why hasn't it happened? Why haven't the people seen what I've been able to accomplish with a bunch of cheap, broken-down horses and given me a chance with some really good ones?"

He rubbed his thumb absently over hers. "Hell, Jess, who knows? All I can tell you is what my mama preached to us all our lives."

"What's that?"

"If it's meant to be, it will be, when the time is right. If not, who knows what God might have planned for you that's better?"

Jessie contemplated his words. "That makes it sound as if it doesn't matter how hard you try—you might not make your goals."

"That's right."

She shook her head. "It isn't fair."

He gave her another smile. "Mama also says that life is a lot of things, but it isn't always fair."

Jessie stared down at their linked hands, her mind returning to Dan's phone call.

"I don't want to lose Cissy," she said, lifting her eyes, awash with tears, to his. "Life wouldn't be that unfair, would it?"

"No."

"You're sure?" she asked in a quavering voice.

"Yes."

As she had done when he arrived, Jessie went into his waiting arms, this time letting her sorrow flow freely in tears that dampened the front of his shirt.

He'd never seen her so... undone. Never seen her when she wasn't in control of the situation and her emotions. Her agony was heartrending, unnerving, even frightening. A feeling of total inadequacy flooded him. He didn't know what to do to help someone who'd always disdained his help. He couldn't think of any words of comfort. All he could do was hold her, press kisses to the top of her shining hair and caress her with loving hands.

Jessie didn't know how long she cried, but gradually some part of her mind registered the fact that Bodie's hands were caressing her back. It felt right. Good. And she wondered why on earth she had given up this man for a pipe dream. Was her futile search for herself reason enough to give up his love?

Jessie answered her own mental questions. She'd thought so. She hadn't known who she was, and she had been so afraid of being absorbed by his strength... the very strength that drew her to him. So many years had passed, and she was no closer to knowing who Jessie Harper was than she had been back then. But now, in his arms, it was easy to believe that they could have been happy—even with her insecurities—and that they might have another chance...

In an unpremeditated gesture, she pressed her lips to his neck and lifted her hands to sift through the silky thickness of the dark hair that grew too long on his neck. The action checked the movement of his hands and stopped his breathing.

She chained kisses around his throat and, finding the hollow at its base, delved into it with the tip of her tongue. His low growl of pleasure was her only reward. With shaking fingers she loosened one button of his shirt and nosed the collar aside, planting a row of kisses along his collarbone and inhaling the heady combination of spicy after-shave and the end-of-the-day scent of a hardworking man. A unique Bodie smell.

"Jess..." He groaned her name on a soft expulsion of air and slid his hands up to cradle the back of her head. Grasping her braid, he tugged slightly and brought her head back. Jessie's eyes fluttered open and she looked up at him with surrender in her eyes. A sweet surrender that kicked his heartbeats into high gear and sent the blood singing through his veins. Ever so slowly, he lowered his head, giving her the opportunity to back out of the kiss if she wanted. Instead, her fingers tightened on his head, pulling it lower until his lips touched hers.

The kiss was soft, tentative, searching and totally unlike the possessive assault of his lips the day he'd first returned. His opened mouth closed over hers, swallowing her sigh of submission and savoring the honeyed nectar of her mouth. Then, drawing a deep breath and pulling Jessie closer simultaneously, he tilted his head and slanted his lips over hers again.

Her hands were crushed between them, and all she could do was insinuate two of her fingers between the buttons of his shirt, brush them against the warmth of his bare skin and marvel at how the world and her problems disappeared the moment his lips found hers.

Nothing mattered. Not the past. Not Dan. Not Cissy. She knew there was forgetfulness in his arms, rebirth when his body took hers, giving her back a new sense of self—a Jessie Harper who was better, prettier, more fulfilled. Jessie Harper, a woman who could make this manliest of men purr with satisfaction. With his body merged with hers, she could find herself and a surcease of every pain. Wanting throbbed in the very heart of her. A wanting that grew as his mouth tasted hers with soft, nibbling, openmouthed kisses that touched the corners of her mouth and tugged at her bottom lip with a gentle suckling motion that sent her blood pressure skyrocketing.

Then he touched her.

Shifting slightly to put more room between them and wedging his leg between hers, he found her breast and his thumb began a slow rotation around her cresting nipple. Her shirt and the delicate wisp of her bra—one of her few concessions to femininity—might well have been nonexistent. Jessie's breath hung suspended on a heartbeat and she gripped handfuls of his shirt to steady her spinning world.

Bodie lifted his lips from hers and drew back; their eyes meshed, mated, as their bodies had done so often in the past. Not bothering to hide the slumbering sexuality lurking in the moss-green depths of his eyes, Bodie moved to the buttons of her shirt, paused and when he met no resistance, began a purposeful unanchoring of each one. To his surprise, Jessie began to do the same to his.

Finished, she peeled the soft fabric off his shoulders and he shrugged out of it, tossing it to the floor. Then he put his arm around her shoulders and led her to the sofa. Lowering her onto it, he parted her blouse, revealing the golden tan of her skin and the meager, lacy barrier that was all that hid her.

She waited for him to slide his hands beneath her, but instead, he slipped his fingers beneath the top edge of her bra, inching the flimsy filament downward. She could feel the backs of his fingertips against her nipples as the rosy tips came slowly into view. Still he tugged, turning his fingers and running them inside the cloth and lifting until her breasts slipped their silken bondage and were fully exposed to his heated gaze.

She saw him swallow, his throat working convulsively. Watched his eyes close as if the sight before him were too much to take.

"Please..." The sound of her pleading voice brought his gaze back to hers, and her hands lifted to his face, which was covered with stubble, cradling it with loving tenderness. Bodie read the age-old message in her eyes, and his head began a downward movement. Jessie's hands slid from his cheeks, winnowing through the thick vibrancy of his hair. Slowly, slowly, his head lowered...

The first touch of his lips loosed a soft gasp from her throat. Her hands tightened, anchoring him to her. When his lips parted and his tongue curled around the sensitive peak of her breast, drawing it into the warm, wet cavern of his mouth, Jessie instinctively arched against the hardness of the torso between her legs, searching for a closeness that couldn't bridge the barrier of denim between them.

He laved, kissed, suckled. His tongue stroked, his lips nuzzled and, with an exquisite gentleness, his teeth worried the sensitive tip and the soft undersides of her breast. Then, fairly, rightly, deliberately, he transferred his attention to the other.

Her breath came in shallow gasps, a soft panting interspersed with sharply indrawn breaths and softly uttered moans that fell on his ears like a benediction. Nothing had changed. The passion that had always raged between them was alive and well and, if anything, hotter than it had ever been. He needed to see it and lifted his head, despite her low protest.

He wasn't disappointed. The desire was there, burning brightly in her dark eyes. He touched one pink and pouting nipple with his forefinger and each callused finger in turn, then thumbed the wet lubricity left by his kisses in slow, concentric circles.

"I want you." His confession rasped from his throat, from his heart, from his very soul.

Jessie's answer was in the arms that reached for him, in the way her body leaned toward his, in the affirmation glowing from her eyes.

His breath and his will rippled from him in a long sigh that wound out from his lungs. Jessie's tongue darted out and slicked across her lips; Bodie bent to take them, but before his mouth could claim hers, she whispered, "Make me forget, Bodie...about Cissy and Dan...and..." Her voice trailed away at the precise instant his body stiffened beneath her hands. "Bodie? What is it?"

He dropped his head without answering. He couldn't. It was the final blow in a series he'd received at this woman's hand. Her words were devastating, unendurable and doused his desire as effectively as cold water roused a fainting person. She didn't really want him. She only wanted what he could make her feel, a few moments of forgetfulness in his arms, not the lifetime of loving he wanted to give her. She wanted to take, not share.

How much more pain could she possibly inflict? he wondered. Better yet, how much more was he willing to take? At that moment, none. He started to move away, but her hand clutched at his arm.

"Bodie? What is it?"

"I've changed my mind, Jessie."

Her face held the question she voiced. "Why?"

Rising from the sofa, he bent and reached for his shirt before answering. His voice throbbed with pain and suppressed desire. "Because I don't want you this way."

He didn't want her. He didn't want her. Her mind chanted the words over and over. How stupid of her to think he did. For the first time ever, she was embarrassed by her state of seminudity and drew her shirt over her breasts. She struggled to sit up. In a token defense against her mortification, she asked angrily, "Then what was all this about—to see if you could still make me want you? Is it some sort of test? Revenge? What?"

"It was none of those, damn it!" he snapped, reaching the end of his tether and finishing with the last button of his shirt. He unsnapped his pants. The zipper ground downward and he shoved the tail of his shirt inside. "I want you to make love because you want me, because you think we have something together. Not as some sort of anesthesia against the pain another man is causing you. I don't want you that way."

She watched as he zipped his pants, snapped the snap and ran the palm of his hand over the fly to smooth it flat in a routine masculine gesture that robbed her of breath and her anger, leaving her with an aching void of desire. Her tongue skimmed her dry lips. "Bodie, please..."

Putting his hands on his hips in a manner that underscored his disgust, he stared down at her, ignoring the hurt in her eyes. "Please what, Jessie? Go? Stay? What? I don't know what you want from me, anymore. One day you're asking me to get out of your life, the next you're begging me to stay...to make love to you to help you forget your problems."

He was right, and her indecision wasn't fair. But she still hadn't sorted out all her feelings for him. She only knew that she couldn't bear for him to leave her. "You don't have to make love to me," she told him. "Just hold me."

It was what he wanted to hear, but the soft, begging voice couldn't penetrate the pain her former plea had caused. Knowing he'd be sorry later and unable to fight a growing despair, he heard his voice—a voice that sounded hard and uncaring—say, "I'm sorry, Jessie, but at the moment, I just don't feel that damned noble."

Chapter Six

Bodie left with a grinding of gears, a spraying of loose gravel and a mild curse, battling the demons of hurt that warred with his love and tore at his soul. Jessie had robbed him of his masculinity with one fell blow, even while the wistfulness and hurt in her eyes damned him for being a selfish clod. In one way or another, Jessie Harper promised to be his undoing.

He wondered if she had kept Dan Givens as confused as she did him. As usual, thoughts of Dan brought out the worst in Bodie. The man was a thorn in his flesh, a gouge to his self-worth. He'd been Jessie's husband, fathered Jessie's child. And Jessie was his. Bodie Lattimer's. Why couldn't she recognize it, when it was something he'd known from the first time he'd seen her, just over seven years ago?

She and Vera had been new to Louisiana racing, bringing their hard-luck Florida stock to a new place in hopes of changing their luck. Jessie had only been twenty-three the first time he'd seen her. It was one of his rare excursions to the grandstand, and he was standing at the chain-link fence along with the other railbirds because his father was running a horse in the same race. But instead of watching his dad's horse, he became interested in Jessie. Wearing a turquoise and apricot satin windbreaker monogrammed with the stable's name, she was saddling a horse in the paddock, her long mane of silky blond hair twisted into a knot on top of her head.

But the thing that had impressed him, the thing he still remembered after so long, was her confidence. Her filly was nervous, wild-eyed and drenched in sweat. Washing out was common enough, but the way she handled the filly was impressive. Calm, collected and obviously knowledgeable, she'd talked constantly, running her hands over the mare's quivering flesh while the identifier checked her tattoo and the valet went through the saddling procedure.

Taken with the regal aura she projected, he'd fallen into step beside her and Vera and introduced himself after the horses had gone to the track. He told them it looked as if the horse were fighting the bit and asked if they'd had her teeth worked on lately.

When Jessie had turned the full impact of her brown eyes on him, smiled a warm smile and proceeded to ask him some pertinent questions about his credentials, he was lost . . . and had been ever since.

His palm hit the steering wheel in an unsatisfactory attempt to vent his frustration. Damn it! Maybe com-

ing back was a bad move. After all, just because he
still wanted Jessie didn't mean she still wanted him.

But she does.

He knew that much for certain. The truth of the
matter was that maybe she didn't love him, maybe she
never had. But she wanted him. Then and now. Her
response a few moments earlier was real.

He tried to close his mind to the pictures playing
relentlessly on the screen of his memory—the way her
mouth had opened to the searching probe of his
tongue, the way her sighs had spoken of her own
arousal. The way her pouting breasts filled his hands
and the warm woman smell of her filled his senses.

That hadn't been his imagination, as the most masculine part of his body still attested. But having her
physically just wasn't enough and it never would be.
He wanted Jessie heart-whole, and wholeheartedly
giving of herself. Sometimes, as now, he wondered if
it was all worth it. He wondered if his quest for her
love was futile, senseless. But when he remembered the
way she had responded to him, the way she had rushed
to him for comfort and begged him to stay, he still felt
a flickering flame of hope that refused to be snuffed
out.

He turned onto the street of the prestigious subdivi-
sion where his brother, Cary, lived and where he'd been
staying the past few days while his houseboat was being
repaired. Resolving to give her just one more chance
and cursing the bit of optimism that kept him doggedly
to his resolve to get her back, he shoved the gear shift
into park. Sometimes, he thought grimly, determination was as much a curse as it was a blessing.

* * *

Jessie watched him leave with wide, disbelieving eyes. Disbelief that slowly changed to anger. How could he turn his feelings off and on that way? How could he be so sweet and tender one minute and scathing and hurtful the next? And what had she said to bring about such a change?

Make me forget... Cissy... Dan... She reconstructed the scene in her mind and it obligingly played back her words.

I don't want you this way.

What way? This was where she got lost. And then it hit her.

Pride. That wretched, masculine pride. Understanding at last what caused his change of heart enabled her to see things through his eyes. She could see now how he might interpret her plea as he had, and how he would consider it just another slap in the face. She could see how, to Bodie, this was just another in a long string of rejections dealt by her hand.

Regret pulled at her heartstrings. How could she make him see that she hadn't meant it that way? That she had wanted him? Should she even try? She doubted if he would come back on his own this time and realized with a start that she might finally be getting her wish for him to stay out of her life. The realization brought a sharp ache to her heart that she didn't understand. After all, that was what she wanted. Wasn't it?

By Sunday she wasn't so sure. Francine brought Cissy back home on Sunday night, as promised. Dan's threat was never mentioned. The handing over of her daughter had been a moment of supreme happiness for Jessie, who worried that in spite of all assurances to the contrary, her days with the child were numbered. Francine was polite, but her usual smile was gone and Jessie thought she detected a trace of pity in her eyes. Neither brought up the subject that was uppermost on their minds as Cissy raced to Jessie and threw her arms around her legs. Francine didn't mention picking Cissy up on Friday and Jessie didn't either.

By Wednesday, she had begun to think that the night was her enemy. Bodie was working several farms in the area, so she couldn't even attempt to explain things to him. Sleep was a thing of the past. Tears—a commodity that had been in short supply in her life—were now abundant. She cried for Cissy. And for herself and Bodie, and all she'd so willfully tossed aside so she could learn who Jessie Harper was. She reasoned that if she hadn't listened to Vera and had been more secure in herself, none of what she was going through would have happened. But reasoning and hindsight didn't change things.

Thankfully, the day was busy, and there was little time left to feel sorry for herself. After running second in the last race and making the obligatory stop at the spit barn, Jessie led the horse back to their barn, her mind once again torn between worrying about Cissy and Bodie and wondering just how much more she could take. She stepped into the shedrow, which was shaded by canvas stretched top to bottom over two by fours as an awning. Her eyes were struggling against the sudden dimness after their exposure to the blinding afternoon sunshine when she heard a questioning, masculine voice ask, "Are you Jessie Harper?"

Straining to focus on the man standing no more than thirty feet from her—someone looking for a trainer, she surmised—she uttered an affirmative, "Yes."

The man began to move toward her. There was absolutely nothing in his manner to cause alarm, but the hair on her nape rose in sudden and irrational apprehension. A tall man, he was dressed in a suit that spoke of money in a quiet, tasteful way. His nearness and her light-adapted eyes finally meshed and she got her first really good look at him. Jessie paled. His face was achingly familiar. Even though she couldn't remember ever seeing him personally, she'd seen his still attractive, lined face several times in the Florida papers as one of the state's most prestigious sons. Dear God, it couldn't be...

"I'm Merle Harper, Jessie. Your father."

All the air in the shedrow, perhaps the world, was suddenly sucked away by a giant vacuum. She couldn't breathe. She couldn't speak. All she could do was stand on legs that threatened to fold beneath her and stare in utter disbelief at the man who had deserted her twenty-seven years before.

Selfish. No good. A womanizer. Vera's pithy descriptions of Merle Harper roared in her ears. The horse snorted and stomped with impatience, but the fact barely registered. Anger, some part of her mind reminded her. *You're supposed to be angry.*

But instead of anger, she felt numbness. It was hard to be angry looking into a face that was as devoid of color as she knew hers was. It was hard to face him with fury blazing in her eyes when his eyes, brown like hers, were filled with sorrow, regret . . . anxiety. Anxiety that she recognized teetered on the edge of downright fear.

She gripped the lead shank tighter and her brows drew together in question. Why should he be afraid?

"I wanted to see you."

The words shocked her almost as much as seeing him had. She drew in a breath that tore at her throat and lungs, more a gasp of disbelief than a natural indrawing of air. Unable to dredge up any hurt or defiance in the face of his honesty and swamped with nothing but a feeling that the moment wasn't real, but only a slice of surrealistic time, she could only murmur, "Why?"

Merle's Adam's apple worked in his throat. He ushered a tight smile to his lips. "Why don't you put the horse up? Then maybe we can talk."

Taking his advice, she put the horse in the stall and began to remove the saddle. Talk. What could they possibly have to talk about after twenty-seven years— except, she thought with a bit of Vera's bitterness, why he'd waited so long to look her up? They had no mutual friends, no interests . . . nothing.

Sighing, she carried the bridle and saddle to the tack room, aware that the man who said he was her father followed her inside. Out of the corner of her eye she saw him scrub a shaking hand over his face, a gesture that betrayed the fact that he was as upset as she was. As she hung up the bridle he plunged his hands into the pockets of his slacks and asked, "Would you like to go somewhere for dinner?"

Jessie whirled around. ''No.'' The word was spoken too quickly, too loudly. If she could think of nothing to say now, she certainly couldn't maintain a conversation over such a lengthy period. Still, the disappointment on her father's face sent a shaft of remorse through her.

''I . . . I have to pick Cissy up from the sitter's,'' she placated.

''Cissy?''

''My daughter.''

Pain seared his face. Regret lurked in his eyes. His voice held the thickness of feelings held prisoner. ''I . . . didn't know. You're married then?''

Jessie shook her head. ''Divorced.''

Fresh sorrow deepened the lines already in his face. ''Divorce is . . . hard. On . . . everyone. I'm sorry.''

She could see that he was. Was he thinking of himself and Vera, and now, after all this time, how their divorce might have hurt their child? ''So am I.''

Silence reigned for a moment, and then, because they didn't have anything to say to one another, and because the question had burned inside her for so many years, she asked, ''What happened?''

His smile was wistful, sad. ''It's a long story, and you need to go.''

He was giving her an out, but Jessie had to know. She had to have something to compare to Vera's point of view. Had to see how the stories meshed. She wanted to know at whose feet to lay the blame for her parent's split. In spite of the myriad conflicting emotions battling for supremacy inside her, and knowing she was letting herself in for more pain, she asked,

"Would you like to go with me to get her? We can stop and get some hamburgers to take home."

Her father's smile was slow, thankful and, to any observer, very much like Jessie's own. "Thanks," he told her. "I'd like that."

They choreographed the move to Jessie's place, Merle opting to follow Jessie in his rental car, which was just as well since he had a hard time controlling the onslaught of emotion that clotted his throat and brought the sting of remorseful tears to his eyes when Cissy bounded down the steps of the small residential house beside her mother, a carbon copy of Jessie as he remembered her.

After that, the trip to the trailer park—via McDonald's—didn't take long, and they were soon pulling into the driveway. Jessie had taken the opportunity during the drive to explain who Merle was to her daughter, but when Cissy asked why he hadn't come to see them sooner, she had been at loss for an answer.

Then, amid much trepidation and slamming of doors, they got out of their cars, and Merle faced his granddaughter for the first time. Cissy stood looking up at the tall man, sizing him up in much the same way she'd taken Bodie's measure the first time she'd seen him. Merle waited, his eyes never leaving the little girl's piquant face.

"What took you so long to come?"

For long seconds, he just stood looking down at her with a look of contrition in his eyes—a well-dressed man who wore a designer suit and a mantle of guilt. Strangely, the guilt fit him as poorly as the expensive suit hanging from his large frame. "I guess the time just slipped away from me."

Cissy thought about that a moment. She'd heard the adults in her life use the excuse more than once. The answer, though not fully comprehended, was acceptable. Holding out her hand, she said, "Come on in, Grandpa. I want to show you what I bought my mom."

Placing his hand in hers, Merle allowed himself to be led to the front door. His eyes, when they met Jessie's, were filled with the glimmer of tears and a barely discernible joy.

Jessie led the way inside and began to bustle around, putting the hamburgers and fries on plates and filling glasses with ice. "I hope you like what I got," she said, realizing that she hadn't asked his preference.

Merle smiled, a motion that crinkled his cheeks upward. "It doesn't matter. It will be fine."

She pulled three napkins from the napkin holder and, with a final survey of the table, said, "Well, here it is."

The meal went surprisingly well, since by unspoken agreement, Jessie and Merle postponed any serious talk until after Cissy went to bed. Cissy's bubbly personality and the fact that her grandfather was showering her with attention covered any possible awkwardness. Before they finished, Merle was laughing so hard at some of Cissy's antics that Jessie found a smile on her lips as well.

It was funny, she mused. All her life she had been programmed to hate this man. Yet watching him with Cissy made that a hard task. Loneliness radiated from him in huge waves and, when he offered to play a game with Cissy after dinner and sat still, waiting for her response, there was a vulnerability hiding in the shadows of his eyes that couldn't be ignored. It was as if he expected her to turn him down, as if he were waiting for her to say no.

He glanced up and met Jessie's eyes. There, in the pain-racked depths of his, she saw the beasts she battled daily. The need to be recognized as someone, to have an importance in someone's life...a lack of self-worth. A plea for a love he had let get away from him when the woman he had loved left, taking his child and the love she would have given him away at the same time.

"I'm all finished!" Cissy cried, shattering the visual reaching and searching between father and daughter. "Let's play!"

Jessie sat on the edge of her chair and watched while Merle played games with Cissy for thirty minutes. She wanted to hear his story. The need ate at her, but she couldn't deny him Cissy's company when they were both so obviously enjoying the game and one another. Any fool could see that Merle's need to be accepted was as great as hers to know.

Finally, amid Cissy's whining protests, Jessie managed to get her daughter bathed and tucked into bed. When Cissy demanded that her grandfather be with her when she said her prayers, Jessie left the room. The quivering of Merle's lips were her undoing as the empathy she felt for him made a subtle mutation to the first tender shoots of love that circumstance had denied them.

She fixed a pot of coffee and put two mugs on the Formica-topped bar that delineated the living room and kitchen. When Merle stepped into the room a few minutes later, he was wiping his eyes with a handkerchief. Noticing Jessie watching him, he hastily wiped his nose and plunged the cotton square into his pocket.

"She's absolutely delightful," he said with a hesitant smile.

"Thank you." Jessie smiled in return. "She can be a handful."

"You always were, too."

Smiles froze on both faces at the casual mention of a hurtful past. Jessie broke the silence by asking, "Would you like a cup of coffee?"

"Please."

Merle seated himself at the bar and added two spoonsful of sugar to the fragrant brew she set before him. Jessie sat down and both of them became inordinately interested in the dark, steaming liquid.

"Would I know her father?" he asked at last.

Jessie shook her head. "No. Dan isn't from the racing community. His family is from Bradley, Arkansas. Respectable pillars of the community. They owned a lot of farmland, and someone drilled an oil well that hit really big. Before they knew it, they were looking for a tax write-off and Dan approached Mother and me to get him some horses."

"And it was love at first sight?"

Jessie looked up. "No. Actually, I married him on the rebound. I didn't really love him the way I should have."

Silence descended on them and both of them became wrapped up in their memories. Finally, Merle cleared his throat. "Your mother and I met in much the same way," he said at last. "My father approached your grandfather about training some horses for him.''

Without waiting for her to comment, he went on. ''She was the prettiest thing I'd ever seen, with those dark eyes and that long brown hair. I was totally captivated.''

A wistful smile curved his mouth and lit his eyes. ''I was used to debutantes whose biggest accomplishment was shopping for clothes and deciding what to wear to a party—helpless, simpering girls who couldn't even balance a checkbook. Your mother was different. She was vivacious, smart as a whip and ambitious. She was going places.''

Just like me.

''I had to have her,'' Merle continued, ''so I asked her to marry me. My parents were furious, of course. Her background wasn't good enough. She didn't have the breeding they wanted. But for once in my life, I didn't back down. I loved her, Jessie.''

Aware of every nuance of feeling that crossed his features, Jessie saw the truth in his eyes. She sipped at her coffee and waited for him to continue.

''She *was* out of the league of my family and their friends, but she tried. She was smart, and it didn't take her long to catch on to all the so-called social graces.'' He sighed. ''She might as well have been eating her peas with a knife for all the good it did. They wouldn't give her a chance, no matter how hard she tried. They'd made up their minds to shut her out, and they did a damn good job of it.''

For the first time, Jessie hurt for all the abuse her mother must have taken from his family. ''Why didn't you take up for her?''

"I did at first. And then we found out you were on the way. I know Vera thought—hoped—that you would help make us a stronger team. She even begged me to take you both away and start over, but I wouldn't listen." His voice was rife with self-loathing. "I'd never had to work for anything in my life and the prospect scared me to death. So we went on like we were."

Pausing in his story, Merle took a drink of his coffee. His eyes held a faraway look. "They never let up. When I went to the office, it was my father gouging about her racetrack background. If I went to see my mother, she ranted about Vera's inability to fit in with their friends and associates.

"I started to drink, just to take the edge off my frustration, but that only made things worse." He scrubbed at his face and brought his gaze back to Jessie. "I began to get tired of arguing to defend her. It was easier to just listen to them rant and rave and then go get drunk to forget. Your mother and I began to fight about my drinking, and that just gave me more reason to do it."

He looked directly at her and aimed his final arrow of hurt. "Bars are a good place to meet women, Jessie...and there were several before your mother finally got fed up and left me."

It seemed to Jessie that he said it deliberately—whether to clear the air between them once and for all or to drive the final wedge between them, she wasn't sure. He sat waiting, the same look on his face she'd seen there when he'd waited for Cissy's decision about playing after dinner. But Jessie knew about the women, so his confession didn't move her. "I know about them," was all she said.

Visibly surprised by the way she took his announcement, Merle grew silent and thoughtful. "She hated the drinking and the women," he said at last, "but I think what finished us off is the fact that I stopped taking up for her. I stopped telling her I cared."

He forced himself to look at Jessie eye to eye. "Maybe by that time, I didn't. I don't know. I didn't stand up for what I wanted, so I lost it. The blame for our marriage failing is mine. And I'm sorry I let it happen."

No one could doubt the sincerity Jessie saw shining on his face. Not even her mother, if she could see it. Jessie felt the sting of tears beneath her eyelids. She'd heard Vera's version of her marriage and its demise many times, with Merle portrayed as the villain. But now she saw the other side, and realized something that Vera's hurt and rejection had blinded her to. Merle was a victim of his family's dominance and rigid social structures. He'd been pampered, smothered and never allowed to think for himself, never permitted to make any relevant personal decisions that would help him grow into an emotionally mature person. Jessie perceived him as a victim, not a villain.

She put her hand on the countertop. Merle took it in his, his fingers squeezing tightly. Neither spoke. Neither could. They just sat and smiled at each other through a glaze of tears.

Twenty minutes later, Merle Harper left his daughter's house. He pulled out of the driveway onto the blacktop street, his heart lighter than it had been in years. As he started down the street, he passed a pickup truck with a woman driving. As he went by, she turned to look at him. He noticed that though she was attractive, with a silver streak through her hair, there was a bitter twist to her lips.

All Vera saw was a gray-haired man whose red-rimmed eyes and drooping shoulders projected a weary defeat that aged him unfairly.

"Who was that?" Vera asked Jessie a few moments later.

Jessie turned, whisked up her father's coffee cup and set it in the sink, wondering how to break the news of Merle's visit. Then she got a clean cup and poured Vera a full cup of coffee, more to stall for time than anything else.

"Well," Vera prompted when Jessie didn't answer immediately, "who was it?"

Deciding, like her father, to stand her ground just once, Jessie turned and said, "That was your former husband. My father."

"Merle?" Vera's eyes were round with shock. "What did he want?"

Jessie shrugged and set Vera's coffee in front of her. "Just to see me, I guess. He didn't really say."

Anger pushed aside the surprise on Vera's face and replaced it with warm color. "He just wanted to see you? Damn the gall of the man!"

I don't need this, Mother. Not now. Not with Dan threatening to take my baby away and Bodie walking out of my life for probably the last time. "What's the matter with him wanting to see me?"

Vera's eyes were disbelieving. "What's the matter? Good Lord, Jessie! After twenty-seven years of silence from him, do you even have to ask?"

Jessie felt her own anger—along with a sense of futility—rising at Vera's predictable response. "He isn't what you said he was."

"No? Then why did he desert us?"

"He didn't! You left him!" Jessie cried.

"Yes, I did. And for a lot more reasons than you know!" Vera ranted. "He's a user, Jessie. He's getting older and his past is haunting him. He's only come to see you and try to get in your good graces to salve what conscience he has left."

Bodie, I need you. If only she could draw on the comfort she knew she could get from him. If only... Lacing her fingers tightly together and drawing a less-than-calming breath, Jessie struggled for control. Fighting with Vera would do no good. She had to try to reason with her.

"I'm sure you're right, Mother. It must have been devastating for you at the time, but—"

"But Merle has managed to come in here and play on your sympathies."

"He isn't like that!" Jessie almost shouted.

"Oh? You're an expert on the man after seeing him once?"

"Of course not! But if you could see how he was with Cissy..."

"Cissy! You let him see my granddaughter?"

Jessie's tenuous control snapped. Fury flooded her. As usually happened when she was consumed by anger, Jessie grew utterly calm. "Yes. He saw Cissy—his granddaughter. We had hamburgers together. They talked. They played a game. He tucked her in. And then *we* talked. He told me his version of what happened..."

"All lies, no doubt."

"Mother, will you listen to—"

"Are you seeing him again?"

"Of course, I'm seeing him again. I'd like to get to know him."

"Why? He's never cared to get to know you before now."

"I know, but—"

"I can't believe this," Vera muttered darkly. "I can't believe that after all I've done for you, you're taking his side." It was a statement, not a question.

"There is no side to take!" Jessie told her, watching in shock as her mother rose and started for the door. "Mother! Come back here! We're adults, for goodness sake!"

Vera never slowed her pace.

Jessie's head moved from side to side in negation. How could she, or anyone else, ever break through the bitterness?

At the door, Vera turned. If it weren't too absurd to believe, Jessie thought she saw a hint of hurt in her eyes. "I can't believe that you fell for his lies."

"Actually, Mother, it was the same story you told me," Jessie said. She didn't add that Merle took sole blame for the breakup of their marriage. There was no need. Vera hadn't heard a word she'd spoken. She couldn't have heard for the sound of the door slamming shut.

Jessie sank down into a kitchen chair, her trembling hands creeping up to cover her lips. What else could possibly happen? She felt the overwhelming urge to cry again, but forced the damnable tears back and tried to reason out her newest predicament. She was caught between a rock and a hard place.

She loved Vera, in spite of how hard she sometimes was to love. And she owed her so much. But it wasn't fair for her to set unspoken ultimatums. It wasn't right for her to deny Jessie knowledge of her father, no matter what had happened between them. She had a right to make her own judgments about people—no matter who they were. And that included Bodie.

Jessie dropped her head into her hands. Bodie. Where was he? What would he think about her father coming back? She wanted to call him. Needed to. But would he want that after Friday night? Or was he finished with her for good?

Chapter Seven

By Thursday evening, Bodie was as miserable as he'd ever been. His first reaction when he'd left Jessie Friday was to go out and get dog drunk, but he'd learned the hard way that drinking didn't solve anything. And the more he thought about it, the more he regretted the way he'd left her Friday night. He'd known how vulnerable she was, how upset Dan's threat had left her. But damn it, she'd thrown his love back in his face one too many times!

Love takes and takes. His mother's words slipped through his mind. *And it never loses hope.* She was right. He'd come back to Louisiana for Jessie because he loved her, and sometimes he was convinced that she still felt something for him, too. Now wasn't the time to quit. He reached into his pocket for his keys and heaved a sigh of surrender, knowing he wouldn't be finished with her until she sent him away forever and made him believe she meant it.

Bodie reached her house in fifteen minutes. He knocked on the trailer door and plunged his hands into his back pockets while he waited. His summons was answered in a matter of seconds when Jessie opened the door and stood looking up at him with wide, surprised eyes. They stared at each other, neither speaking, for what seemed to Bodie an eternity. Would she forgive him?

Will he ever forgive me? Jessie looked up into his face, seeing the lines of weariness the sleepless nights had etched there, seeing the sorrow and apprehension in his eyes. When would they stop hurting one another? Then she was somehow in his arms, her face against his chest, listening to the slow, steady beating of his heart and feeling him press kisses to the top of her head.

"I'm sorry, Jessie. I'm an insensitive bastard for leaving you like that the other night," he told her in a voice riddled with self-disgust.

"No!" she hastened to correct him, pulling back and looking up at him. "It's my fault."

She rested her cheek against him again and held him tightly, realizing she had learned a lot in the course of a few weeks and a lifetime of lessons in the past few hours. Bodie coming back had set off a chain of events that had disrupted her life and challenged her dreams and aspirations. Her goals and ambitions—the things that had seemed so important at twenty-three—paled in significance now that she realized what they had cost her. Her problem with Dan and her father's untimely arrival only sharpened the contrast of what she had actually done with her life when compared to her lofty dreams.

Meeting Merle and hearing his side of the story had put things into focus for her. It had made her able to distinguish the dross from the gold. And for that—and in spite of the scene with Vera—she would be eternally grateful.

Releasing Bodie at last, she took his hand and led him inside. He closed the door behind them, but when she tried to lead him to the sofa, he stopped her with a gentle, resisting tug on her hand.

When she turned with a question in her eyes he offered her a slow smile and pulled her to him. But instead of taking her into his arms again, he cradled her cheeks in the palms of his scarred and callused hands, looking down at her as if he wanted to imprint every millimeter of her face on some part of his mind.

Wispy strands of fine, fair hair had come loose from her braided ponytail and lay around her face in disarray. Her face was pale beneath her tan, making the scattering of freckles across her nose more pronounced. She'd been crying, and her eyes, washed free of mascara and rimmed with red, held a new, unexplained contentment. Her lips... Bodie drew in a deep breath. Her lips were lipstick-nude and trembling, asking for the kiss he wanted so badly to give her. He wasn't certain he had ever loved her more.

I don't think I've ever loved him more than I do at this very moment.

The unexpected thought slipped without warning beneath Jessie's guard, her woman's heart taking advantage of her temporary weakness and forcing her intellect to face what it had known all along.

She loved him. Had always loved him. It wasn't, as she'd told him before, just that sex was good between them. That was only a small part of what she felt for him, of what he made her feel.

The realization brought both a sense of jubilation to her heart and a deep feeling of responsibility. Loving someone didn't make everything automatically okay. It wasn't a panacea for every need a person had. It required so many things. Patience. Sacrifice. Total commitment. Love was a tender burden, but a burden that made life worth living.

It came to her slowly, a lesson Vera had never learned. Like all men—all people—Bodie was both good and bad, but the good far outweighed the bad. The world saw the brawler, the drinker, the woman-loving, rambling rake, the man who never stayed in one place for long. But intuition and her knowledge of him told her that there was so much more. There was a depth to him most people didn't see, a depth that Jessie knew few had ever plumbed. Somehow she knew that the woman he loved could spend a lifetime uncovering unexpected things about him that the rest of the world didn't see and might not believe if they did.

The woman he loved.

Her?

He must love her. He hadn't said the words, but he'd come back for her, hadn't he? She was the woman who would reap the bountiful harvest of love he would sow. She was the person who could draw from the vast reservoir of love and strength inside him when her own grew low. She was the woman who would know the healing power of his kiss and the gentle, teasing humor that helped to erase the memory of the bad times. Bodie's love would refurbish her inner need to feel wanted, pretty, desirable . . . more a woman.

She offered him a wide, tremulous smile at the same time she offered him her heart. Before he could respond, she turned her face to press a kiss to the palm of one hand, then slid her arms around his middle and pressed her cheek against his hard chest.

"I love you, Bodie." The whisper-soft words were breathed out on a sigh of sweet surrender.

He went completely still. Even his breathing seemed suspended. "What?"

Jessie lifted her head and looked up into his astonished eyes. "I love you."

The astonishment mirrored in his eyes changed to wariness, disbelief.

"And," she added, "I want you." Before he recovered enough to make a reply, her hands came up between them and she loosened his belt buckle with a deft movement that drove a look of surprise to his face. The look intensified when she unsnapped his jeans and began sliding the zipper down with slow deliberation.

Leaning into him and pushing him back against the door, Jessie rose on tiptoe the fraction it took to put her on an eye-to-eye level with him, turning her palms to rest against the crisp hair that matted his belly. Then, with a premeditation that stole his breath, she fastened her mouth to his and slid her hands beneath the elastic waistband of his underwear, cupping the heaviness of his sex in a brazen gesture born of a too-long abstinence.

She pierced the groan of pleasure that erupted from the depths of his throat with her tongue, which began a mating dance with his, while her hands freed him from his cotton bondage, only to recapture him in a pleasurable prison of silken strokes—an exquisite torture that drove him beyond coherent thought.

Jessie . . . Jessie . . .

Her mouth moved over his, slanting, grinding, needing. A need he fed with a hot hunger that equalled hers as they kissed for long, endlessly long moments in an impossible quest to slake a desire that could never be quenched.

At last Bodie tore his mouth from hers and grasped her hands, stilling their movements. Then, breathing as if he had just finished the Boston Marathon, he scanned the room and rasped, "Where's Cissy?"

Jessie had been through three kinds of hell since his return and, seeing things more clearly since Merle's advent into her life, she was driven by a relentless need to give Bodie back a part of what he gave her, to make up for what she had done to them before and to make him happy in the future.

"She had a fit to spend the night next door with Kelly, and I reluctantly let her." Her smile was slow, teasing. "Suddenly, I'm very glad. I want to make love, Bodie," she told him, lifting herself on tiptoe and pressing against him. Her hips began a slow, seductive movement. "I want to make love because I haven't felt you inside me for so long . . . too long. Because there is no one else on this earth who can make me feel the way you do."

Bodie's heart slammed against his ribs at the frankness of her confession. Without a word, he took con-

trol of the situation before his rapidly deteriorating
control snapped completely and they found themselves making love on the floor. Picking her up as
easily as he would heft a sack of feed, he carried her
toward her room. Jessie twined her arms around his
neck and pressed her lips to his whisker-roughened
cheek. When he got to the trailer's narrow hallway, he
swore and turned sideways.

Her laughter was a soft caress against his ear that he
returned with a heart-stopping smile before pushing
open the door of her room and carrying her to the bed.
He deposited her in its center, shut the door and
turned the lock. Then, in a deliberate gesture, he
stripped off his shirt and peeled the faded Wranglers
over his narrow, masculine hips and hair-dusted legs.

Jessie slipped from her blouse and, unfastening her
own jeans, started to wriggle them over her hips.

"Let me," he said, emotion adding a new depth to
his bass voice.

In response, she lifted her legs and flexed her feet.
Taking the hem of the jeans in his hands, he pulled the
fabric down her long legs and tossed them onto the
floor next to his, leaving only two pale lavender scraps
of tricot and lace to inhibit his view of her.

Jessie reacquainted herself with him with love-filled
eyes. She had forgotten how thick the mat of dark hair
was that swirled over his chest, and she was impressed by the fitness of his body. But there was much
more gray in his hair than when he'd left six years ago.
When he smiled down at her, the whiteness of his teeth
slashing the bold bone structure of his face, the
crow's-feet at the corners of his eyes and the creases in
his cheeks seemed more deeply etched. Even so, there

was no doubt Bodie Lattimer was undeniably a raw, virile man.

A raw, virile man whose nearness made every inch of her woman's body scream for his possession. With eyes held by riveting emotions, Jessie and Bodie each divested themselves of their remaining clothing. And then he was with her on the bed, the weight of his body on hers a long-awaited, often-dreamed-of reality. He rolled them to their sides, the hard heat of him cradled against the mound of her womanhood. Driven by a nagging, sensual hunger that only he could fill, Jessie pushed him to his back and slowly lowered herself onto the throbbing shaft of his manhood.

Her eyes widened, then drifted shut. Mutual moans meshed. She relaxed against him, marveling at how perfectly they fit together and wondering how she could have given this ... him ... up.

Bodie found the end of her braid and removed the rubber band holding it with deft movements. His fingers worked through the thick, honey-tinted strands, separating the braid and finally loosening it by pulling a second band free. Reams of blond hair cascaded over her shoulders and tumbled in silken skeins to his chest, where it mingled in sensual abandon with the crisp, black hair growing there.

She felt his hands on her thighs, his callused palms skimming over the golden softness of her skin and igniting a shimmering excitement where their bodies joined. She opened her eyes to look at him and sought to catch the quicksilver feelings with a slow undulation of her hips that sent Bodie soaring upward in a dizzying crescendo of spiraling sensation.

Blindly she reached for his hands and, as he had so many times before, wove their fingers together. Fingers entwined, she forced his hands back against the comforter, her palms in his hands, the pulse in her wrist beating against his pulse, her forearms resting against the muscular length and darkness of his.

For the moment his body was bound by the golden threads of her hair and held prisoner by her weight, his masculinity captured in the moist heat of her, a captivity he relished. Smiling a smile of unadulterated pleasure, he freed his hands and lifted them to her hair, winding his fingers through the silky curtain and pulling her head down until their lips met. Once. Twice. The third time.

Jessie's hips instigated a lazy rhythm.

Bodie groaned against her mouth and answered with a reciprocal thrust of his own hips. His hands moved to the back of her head as her lips parted over his, and he opened his mouth to the hungry onslaught of her kisses. Time ceased to exist. The world receded. There was nothing but the sounds of labored breathing, deep moans and soft, feminine murmurs of pleasure. Nothing but a man and a woman and a need that transcended the physical and defied all past pain and suffering. Two hearts beat in syncopated harmony; two souls rejoiced in second chances as sweat-slickened bodies struggled together toward the purest pinnacle of pleasure. They reached it simultaneously—as they had always done—with a thrust and parry of hips that hurtled them over the edge of ecstasy and into the shimmering sea of sensation beyond...

Jessie's head dropped back and she heard herself cry out. She thought she heard Bodie chanting her name in a strangled, desire-drenched voice, but it might only have been the sound of her heart beating, chanting out a name of its own... *Bodie. Bodie. Bodie.*

She collapsed against him and he rolled their still-joined bodies onto their sides. His hands cradled her bottom and, striving to hold on to what was left of the moment, his mouth trailed across the zenith of her cheekbone in a series of moist kisses.

Drained, sated, filled with love, they lay front to front and tried to climb back onto the whirling world of reality. When Bodie finally withdrew from her to reach for his cigarettes, Jessie rolled to her back and murmured a halfhearted protest, flinging the back of her wrist up to shield her eyes from the glare of the light.

He smiled at her and shook a cigarette from the package, bringing it to his lips and lighting it with a flick of his lighter. He dragged in a draft of smoke and exhaled it toward the ceiling, while his passion-lazy eyes drifted over her with lethargic slowness.

She was beautiful. More beautiful than he remembered. Her face was thinner, the perfection of its oval shape more pronounced, as were the hollows in the cheeks that only accentuated the classic bone structure of her face. Her lashes—the same lashes that hid her brown eyes with subtle provocation—rested against the golden tan of her cheeks in a silken fringe of black. Her mouth... Dear heaven, her mouth... Her short upper lip was slightly parted from the full, pouting lower lip and, though swollen from their kisses, it was a mouth whose very shape begged to be kissed again.

A soft breath hissed from his lips and his eyes meandered from her face down over her body. Though still slender, motherhood had given a new roundness to her hips, breasts and abdomen, which had once been almost concave. A faint sprinkling of whiskey-tinted freckles was scattered over her chest, and a golden tan covered her except for the places where her swimming suit had blocked the sun's rays. She was gorgeous, perfect. And finally his. There was thanksgiving in the peace flooding his soul.

"I love you, Jessie." The words rumbled from deep inside him and urged her eyes open.

She reached out and placed her palm over his heart. He was warm to her touch. Warm and alive. Just the way she felt for the first time since she'd sent him away.

"I love you, too," she confessed. "And I guess I always have. I was just too stubborn to admit that I was weak enough to need someone."

A hint of sorrow warred with the exultation her confession had started within him. Turning, he stubbed out his cigarette before facing her and taking a strand of her hair in his hand. "Needing someone isn't a sign of weakness, Jessie. What made you think it was?"

Her shoulders moved against the sheets in a shrug. "My mother, I guess. All my life she preached not to lean on anyone, especially any man, because they'd let you down sooner or later."

One side of his mustache lifted in a wry smile. "That's funny. My mama always told us that the people you loved and who loved you back were the ones you could lean on. That's what it's all about."

"I think I'm beginning to see that." Her fingers rubbed back and forth against his chest. "You've never let me down."

"No? Not even Friday night?"

"Not even then. That was my doing. But I've let both of us down."

He waited, knowing he was about to hear the explanation he'd longed for.

"I should have never sent you away," she said, refusing to meet his eyes and plucking at the sheet with a gesture that betrayed her nervousness. "I don't really know why I did, but I think it had something to do with my self-esteem."

"Your self-esteem?"

Jessie looked at him from beneath the ebony fringe of her lashes. "Yes. You were always so sure of yourself, so positive you knew who Bodie Lattimer was, that it intimidated me."

Bodie's face mirrored his perplexity. "Why?"

"Mother told me to never count on anyone but myself, but that was hard, because I was never really certain who Jessie Harper was. I had a father I couldn't remember seeing, no real roots and a very biased opinion of men in general. Until tonight, all I ever knew about my father was what she told me."

"What happened tonight?" he queried. "There's a difference about you I can't explain."

A soft smile lit Jessie's face. "He came to the track this afternoon. To see me."

"Your father?" Bodie asked incredulously.

She lifted her gaze to his. "He wasn't anything like I expected him to be, Bodie. Nothing like Vera told me he was. Oh—" she hurried to explain "—maybe he was a rounder when he was young, but now he's just old and tired...and sorry for what he's done."

"Is that what he told you?"

She nodded. "He blamed himself for everything that went wrong between them."

Bodie's brows lifted. "I wonder what Vera would think about that?"

"She already knows. They passed each other on the street and she asked me who he was. She was furious that he'd come to see me after all this time."

A long, low whistle hissed from Bodie's lips. "I can imagine. What did she say?"

"That he was only on a guilt trip. That she couldn't believe I'd take his side after all she'd done for me."

"Did you take his side?"

"There is no side to take. It's over between them. But at least now I understand why he did what he did. He just wasn't strong enough to stand up for what he wanted, Bodie. And as much as that weakness hurt me and my mother, I can't hate him for it the way she does. If he'd set out to deliberately hurt us it would be different. Does that make any sense?"

"I think so."

"Seeing him made me see how wrong I'd been when I sent you away six years ago, how wrong it was to marry Dan..." Her voice trailed away in remorse. Her eyes shifted from his.

Bodie brushed the wispy ends of the strand of hair he was holding against her rounded chin, his heart aching with a half-dozen-year-old pain. "Why did you marry Dan?"

There was a hint of defiance in her face. "Because of that self-image I was talking about. When you left, I didn't feel so pretty and wanted anymore. I was just plain Jessie Harper. I deliberately set out to see if I could interest him—just to prove to myself that I was somebody. That somebody out there wanted me."

"I wanted you, Jess."

"I know. But you were different. You frightened me."

"Frightened you! Why?"

"Because you were so strong. I couldn't be certain that your strengths wouldn't swallow me up. I was afraid I might lose what little bit of myself I had." She sighed. "I think the reason I married Dan is because some sixth sense told me that there was no way Dan Givens would overshadow me, just the way you say Michelle will never overshadow Sloan." She laughed dryly. "It isn't a very pretty picture I paint of myself, is it?"

"It's honest, anyway," Bodie said, still trying to deal with what she had told him. It was hard to fathom, but knowing Vera, he could easily see how Jessie could have been so mixed up.

"Yes. I'm finally being honest with myself. And you."

"Then..." He hesitated, wanting to know, but afraid to ask. "You didn't love him?"

She met his questioning look squarely. "I told myself I did. I worked hard to convince myself that I did. But it was all just a con game, my own way of rationalizing what I was doing. I married Dan for all the wrong reasons. He represented a stability that marriage to you couldn't give me, something my life lacked. And he married me to get a wife and mother for his children. It just didn't work. His stability wasn't enough for me, and my failure to be a traditional wife destroyed whatever it was he felt for me. And, like my father, I'm willing to take the blame for my marriage failing.''

''It's never only one person's fault when a marriage fails,'' Bodie said.

''Maybe not,'' she told him, ''but ninety-five percent of the blame can be laid at my feet. I never should have married him. In spite of what he's trying to do to me now, Dan Givens deserves more than he got from me. The only thing I don't regret is Cissy. I think I thought that having a child would make me be more what Dan wanted. More like Francine,'' she told him.

''Francine? What's so great about Francine, besides her teeth?''

Jessie smiled up at him. So he'd noticed Francine's disgustingly sunny smile, too. ''She's everything I'm not.''

''Such as?'' he prompted.

''She's an immaculate housekeeper.''

''You run an immaculate shedrow.'' When she glared up at him, he glanced around the cheerful, feminine bedroom. ''Your place looks pretty good, too,'' he added as a teasing afterthought.

''She can cook and bake up a storm.''

''You make a mean apple pie.''

Jessie sighed. ''Frozen crust, canned filling. Francine would never lower herself to a frozen crust and a canned filling.''

"Francine doesn't have the care of a dozen horses, either."

Jessie's brows drew together. "But that's the problem, Bodie. The horses. Dan couldn't understand the importance of me making a name for myself. He resented the time it took away from him."

"Most men would."

"Would you?"

He looked down at her with a burning intensity. "Would I have to?" he parried. "I thought you had things in perspective now and realized what was important to you."

"I do."

"And?"

"You and Cissy are the most important things in the world to me. But," she hastened to add, "I can never give the horses up completely."

His eyes were filled with a tender understanding. "And I wouldn't ask you to. I love you as you are. I don't want to change you."

A burden lifted from her heart. She felt more at peace than she ever had. Just as with Merle, there was much more that needed to be said, but it could wait. They had cleared the air of the most pressing problems between them, and Jessie was suddenly very tired. It had been an extremely long and exhausting day, filled with many surprises. She wanted to sleep, but not until she had proven to Bodie one more time how much she cared. Smiling up at him, she said, "Everyone wants something different. What would you want from me?"

He saw the hint of teasing laughter lurking in her eyes, but the moment was far too serious for teasing.

"I would want you to love me," he told her. "For today and all our tomorrows."

Jessie's smile faded. She reached up and placed her palm against the side of his face. "I will." His head dipped, but before his lips could take hers, she murmured again, "I will."

Mouths met in a kiss of sweet promise that mutated to passion as Jessie brought his hand to her breast. Surprisingly, Bodie ended the kiss, though he didn't move his hand.

"Uh-uh," he said, with a shake of his head.

"Uh-uh what?"

"Not so fast this time. This time I'm going to take my time. I'm going to see if you still like the things you used to."

"Like what?"

One corner of his mustache hiked up. "Like this."

One hand moved with lightning quickness to the delta at the juncture of her thighs. One bold finger moved with unerring, breath-stealing accuracy to the tiny, hidden place that housed a million sensitive nerve endings. Her stomach muscles tensed. She arched against his hand.

"You do still like that, huh?" he drawled teasingly.

"Beast!" she countered.

His finger moved over the gathering moistness in soft, slow circles that drove her wild with wanting. "Beast, am I?"

"No... Yes... Bodie, please..." she panted.

"Please what?"

"Make love to me."

"I am. But this time we do it my way."

And he did. True to his word, he made love to her slowly, sweetly, thoroughly, wooing her with the soft growl of his voice, courting her with the touch of his callused hands, winning her with the practiced touch of his mouth and taking his winnings with the masterful stroking of his body.

It was perfect, but never enough. Just enough. Too much. And worth waiting for, for six long years.

Chapter Eight

Bodie left in the darkest part of the morning, just before dawn and the beeping of Jessie's alarm clock. She stirred when he left the bed, mumbling something he couldn't understand and reaching out to hold him. Smiling, he dropped a kiss to her forehead before pulling on his clothes and letting himself out of her room and her house. The last thing they needed at this stage of the game was for Cissy to find him in her mother's bed again.

The streets were quiet and calm as he drove through the trailer park. The calmness was fitting. It matched the peace and contentment filling him. He would be forever grateful to Merle Harper for coming back into Jessie's life and setting things right between them. Seeing her father and finding out his version about the breakup with Vera had gone a long way toward filling in the gaps of who Jessie Harper was and where she'd come from. And indirectly, it had gone a long way toward filling in the gaps her absence had left in his own life.

A smile that onlookers would classify as silly curved his mouth and lent a glitter of satisfaction to his green eyes. It was hard to believe she was back in his life again. For the first time in years his emotional future looked secure. All because a woman had committed herself and her heart to him.

She was everything he remembered. More. Her mouth was still the same—tender, pliant, willing. And her body still responded to his touch as it always had, with quicksilver reactions that left him feeling awed, shaken and thankful for another chance. When his body had poured out the proof of his love, it had simultaneously emptied him of the residue of bitterness left inside him. He even felt halfway charitable toward Vera this morning.

A truck whizzed by in the fast lane and a horn honked, bringing his thoughts back to the present. As they passed beneath the glow of the 7 Eleven sign, Bodie recognized the truck as one belonging to one of the blacksmiths. He honked back, waved and grinned. God, but it was good to be alive!

The alarm was an unwelcome intruder on Jessie's wonderfully erotic dreams. Dreams of Bodie's mouth on hers, his lips nuzzling her breasts, his hands caressing her while he penetrated the dewy petals of her womanhood. She groaned a protest at the intrusion, rolled over and groped for the button that would end the senseless beeping.

Turning, she opened her eyes and peered through the early-morning darkness while her hands reached out to find him. Empty. The space beside her was empty. There was nothing left of the night but the barely discernible scent of his spicy cologne that lingered on the sheets, the slight soreness between her thighs and the quiet triumph in her heart.

She flipped back the sheet and swung her bare legs to the side of the bed. Rising, she lifted herself on tiptoe and stretched, arching her back with the same satisfaction as a cat who had just lapped up a puddle of spilled cream. She smiled broadly and low, sexy laughter gurgled from her throat. Reaching back, she swept the silken skein of blond hair from her neck, twisting it into a loose knot and securing it with some pins. She headed blithely for the shower, the freedom she felt in being naked negating her first impulse to cover her glowing body with a robe.

She showered, feeling a difference in herself that was nothing short of phenomenal. The night spent with Bodie had done more for her than she could believe. But it was more than knowing she still had his love that had wrought the change. It was also knowing she had the love of her father, even though things had gone wrong between him and Vera.

Vera. If only there were some way to get her and Merle together, Jessie thought. If only he could tell Vera what he'd told her. Maybe, just maybe, if Vera saw him, she would realize just how wrong it was to judge him as harshly as she had. Maybe she could forgive and then forget...

Her mellow mood stayed with her as she got ready for work and while she stopped at a coffee shop for a cup of coffee. It lasted all the way to the track as she sang along with the Gatlin brothers on the radio. It lasted as she plugged the coffeepot in and set their one groom to work.

It lasted until Vera came through the door.

It was funny, Jessie mused, how the human mind could block out things it didn't want to face. She had been so wrapped up in her euphoria she had forgotten the fight with her mother. Forgotten it or deliberately shoved it to the farthest recesses of her mind.

"My, my, aren't you a little ray of sunshine this morning?" Vera said. "Was your visit with your father that great?"

"Yes, it was, and I see you're your usual self, too, Mother," Jessie shot back.

Vera gave her a dark, searching look and couldn't help but notice the change in Jessie as she bustled around the tack room, assembling salt, baking soda, vitamins and all the other ingredients they added to the horse's feed each day. There was a bounce to her step, a lilt in her voice and a latent sexuality gleaming in her eye. Symptoms that hadn't been brought on by Merle's visit.

"You're sleeping with Bodie Lattimer, aren't you?"

Jessie stopped shuffling bottles around and turned to face her mother, defiance and determination in every line of her body. "And if I am?"

"You're a fool!" Vera spat. "Good grief, Jessie! Learn from your mistakes! Don't repeat them!"

"I'm not repeating them!"

"Aren't you?" Vera challenged. "Didn't he leave you six years ago? What makes you think he won't leave you again?"

"Yes, he left me. After I turned down his proposal of marriage because *you* convinced me he was no good for me."

"He still isn't any good for you."

"Why?"

"Because he travels all over the country."

Jessie's hands went to her slim hips. She nodded her head in a mocking gesture. "Well, that cryptic statement certainly clears things up nicely, doesn't it?"

"You know what I'm trying to tell you."

"Oh, yes, Mother, I know, but say it," Jessie goaded, spurred on by her own mounting anger. "Let's get everything out."

"All right. I'll say it. It's real easy to find women on the prowl when your wife is halfway across the country."

"Bodie would never cheat on me."

Vera's harsh laughter rang through the room. "Any man will cheat on you, given half an opportunity."

Jessie's hands fell to her sides and she turned away from her mother's bitterness, shaking her head and fighting a feeling of frustration. It was no use. Vera would never change. Jessie reached for Styrofoam cups and poured two coffees. Turning, she handed one to Vera. Two sets of dark eyes met, Jessie's holding sorrow and the sheen of impending tears, Vera's holding worry and fear—not the anger Jessie expected to find there. It nagged at her, but at the moment she couldn't figure out why.

"I feel sorry for you, Mother," she stated at last.

Vera laughed shortly. "Sorry for me? Why on earth would you feel sorry for me?"

"Because you're a beautiful woman. You're smart. And you have a great deal of love inside you that you won't share. You have so much to offer a man, but you won't give them the time of day."

"I date."

"Sure. You might go out with someone once or twice. But let one of them show any real interest, and you drop them so fast it's scary."

"They're all interested in one thing—how fast they can get you in the sack."

"I don't believe that," Jessie said with a shake of her head. "And even if it's true, all you have to do is let them know you aren't interested in that kind of relationship."

"And then they move on to someone who is."

Jessie shrugged. "Maybe. Maybe not. But if they really care for you, they'll hang around or keep coming back."

"Like Lattimer?"

"Yes. Like Bodie."

Vera sipped at her coffee. "He'll try to change you, just like Merle did me and Dan did you."

"No. Bodie is stronger than Merle, and he could never be as cruel as Dan, or as heartless."

Vera gave a dry smile that crinkled the fine age lines around her eyes. "Dan, heartless? Cruel? I can't imagine that. What's he want to do? Take Cissy away from you?"

The cup of coffee Jessie was holding slipped from her grasp and fell onto the concrete floor, sending a spray of hot, black liquid up over her boots and jeans. The spilled coffee was forgotten as she asked in a voice that was hardly more than a horrified whisper, "How did you know?"

Vera's face blanched. Her anger at Jessie dissolved in the face of a new problem. "I was just being facetious; it was the most heartless thing I thought Dan had in him. Do you mean he really is trying to take Cissy away from you?"

Jessie nodded.

"For God's sake, why?" Vera railed, turning and beginning to pace the small room. She stopped suddenly and turned back to Jessie, who was fiddling with a bit and reins. "Bodie. He knows you're having an affair with Bodie."

"That's about the gist of it," Jessie acknowledged, glad for some reason that her mother knew. Vera might have many faults, she thought, but she was loyal to those she cared about. And she loved Cissy with all her heart. "The only thing is, he used that for the reason before it was actually fact."

"What do you mean?"

"The night before they were to bring Cissy home after she'd spent the week with them, Bodie came to the trailer drunk. I put him on the couch to sleep it off, and I went to my bed. Honest."

Vera remembered clearly. "I believe you. That was the night he fought Sloan Seavers. I was on my way to your house the next morning and saw Bodie walking down the street. I gave him a ride to the track."

Surprise molded Jessie's face. "You did?"

Vera smiled. "Even Bodie ranks higher on my list than Sloan Seavers. So what happened?"

"I left him there while I came to the track. When I got home he wasn't on the couch. I straightened things up, threw the sheets in the hamper and took a shower. I was just getting out when Francine and Cissy got there. Everything was going along fine when I sent Cissy to my room to put away a miniature she'd bought for me. She came out and asked what Bodie was doing in my bed. Needless to say, I wanted to fall through the floor. He'd gone and crawled into my bed after I left for work.''

"You didn't know he was there?"

Jessie sighed. "If I had, would I have sent Cissy in there?"

"Good point. Obviously, Francine told Dan.''

"No. That's the funny part. I kept expecting him to call, but he didn't. Francine came and picked Cissy up last Friday night as usual. Nothing was said. And then, later that night, Dan called and told me that Cissy had told him.''

"Cissy!" Vera exclaimed. "Why would she mention it?"

"Why not? You know how kids are, Mother. They tell everything they know. Cissy likes Bodie, and she was probably just telling Dan all her experiences with him.''

Vera moved her head from side to side. "What did Dan say when he called you?"

"He accused me of sleeping with Bodie and when I denied it he told me I could tell it to the judge. Then he said he would bring Cissy home like he was supposed to, but that it would be the last time.''

"Damn!"

"My sentiments exactly," Jessie said with a sigh.

"Of course you know that the fact you are sleeping with Bodie now doesn't help your case."

"I know. And I didn't plan this. I fought it as long as I could."

Vera's dark brows lifted with skepticism.

Jessie's eyes held her mother's. "I love him, and he loves me. He knows how important my way of life is, and he doesn't want to change me. And I need what he gives me."

"And what's that?"

"Confidence. In myself as a person. In what I can do."

"You've always been confident," Vera said.

"No," Jessie refuted. "*You've* always been confident in me. I was always trying to measure up to who you said Jessie Harper was and what you said she could do. But inside, I was never really sure she could do anything. But I feel more sure of myself when I know Bodie is around." She looked Vera directly in the eye and added, "And seeing Merle helped, too."

"So we're back to Merle, are we?" Vera asked, but surprisingly there was no venom in her voice.

"I guess so."

Vera's breasts lifted on a deep sigh. "I couldn't sleep last night for thinking about things. I guess feeling a certain curiosity about your father is natural, no matter how I feel about him. I guess I shouldn't begrudge him a few hours of your life, since I've had you for twenty-seven years."

Jessie couldn't believe this major concession. Still, she wanted even more. "How *do* you feel about him, Mother?"

It was Vera's turn to meet Jessie's probing gaze. "I don't know," she said with an honesty that surprised them both. "I've hated him for so long for treating me—us—the way he did. And I was furious when I found out you'd seen him, but after thinking things over, I just don't know. I'm finding it hard to work up any animosity. I guess I'm getting old and tired."

"Maybe," Jessie suggested wisely, "you're just tired of carrying that load of hate around."

Vera's smile was weary, sad and edged with wistfulness. "Yeah. Maybe."

"I would never have believed it. She's changed so much." Merle's laughter sounded a bit grim. "But I guess I don't look like I did nearly thirty years ago, either." He squinted against the bright light reflected off the water. "I guess she was upset about me coming back," he commented as the two-story houseboat chugged slowly away from the Camp Joy dock, leaving behind several other houseboats of varying size, Jimmy's Restaurant and a few awed onlookers. The boat was impressive in size as well as color, since it was painted turquoise and black, the same colors as the Lattimer racing silks.

"Yes," Jessie said, watching his expression closely, glad Bodie and Cissy had talked her into asking Merle to join them for the afternoon's outing. Fortunately for Jessie, Bodie had taken Cissy inside with the promise that he'd let her steer the boat once they cleared the cypress trees and were well out into the lake.

"Knowing Vera, I guess she was upset about me coming back."

"You might say that," Jessie said with a grin before she took a long sip of her lemonade.

Merle stared out over the murky tree-dotted water. A crow, sitting on a branch dripping Spanish moss, shrilled a raucous cry. "I've wanted to come after both of you a hundred different times," he confessed.

Jessie couldn't hide her surprise. "Then why didn't you?"

"Because your mother made it very clear when she left that we were finished, that she didn't ever want to see me again and that she didn't want me around either one of you after I'd been with my women. She said that if I did, she'd smear the Harper name all over the papers and make me the laughingstock of Florida. She made a believer out of me."

Jessie thought of the sting of her mother's tongue. "I can believe it."

This new development didn't put Vera in a very flattering light, but Jessie had been through all the misery and fighting she could handle. It would be better to let sleeping dogs lie than to confront Vera with Merle's version of why he hadn't sought her out before. At this point it wasn't important.

"I'm sorry if coming back has caused trouble between the two of you," Merle said sincerely.

"It doesn't matter. There's been bad blood between Mother and me off and on almost all my life. We did have a fight last night, but this morning she had a different attitude. She said she couldn't blame me for wanting to know about you, so I think it's okay with her now. She even seemed more tolerant of Bodie this morning."

"And what's wrong with Bodie?" Merle asked. He and Bodie had been at ease with one another from the beginning, mostly because Merle saw the love in the younger man's eyes every time they found Jessie across the way. Merle knew his daughter had suffered more than her share of unhappiness, and if Bodie Lattimer was the one who put that gleam of pleasure in her eyes, then Merle was for him a hundred percent.

"Mother always thought that because his job takes him all over the country and he's so good-looking, he'd cheat on me the way you did her."

Sadness dulled the gleam in Merle's eyes. "She's wrong. The man is crazy about you. Why haven't you married him?"

Jessie became inordinately interested in the bits of lemon pulp floating in her glass. "He asked me to once."

"What happened?"

"Just what I said. Mother convinced me he was wrong for me and that I wouldn't be happy with him. And I was so intent on making a name for myself that I was afraid that marriage would interfere with what I wanted to do with my life."

"Which is?" Merle prompted.

She leaned back in her chair and stretched out her legs, a wide smile on her face. "I used to have this pipe dream of being the best woman trainer in the country. Unfortunately, I've never been able to get my hands on good enough horses to even begin to reach that goal."

Merle nodded in understanding. "So you let him go and married Dan on the rebound."

"That's about it. I guess I was trying to prove something to myself." She sighed. "Bodie showed up here a few weeks ago and told me he'd come back for me. That he should never have let me go.''

''And was he right?''

She nodded and a blush of happiness stained her cheeks. ''Yes. I love him. I think I always have. And I want us to have a life together.''

''If that's what will make you happy, baby, then do it,'' Merle urged. ''Don't let anyone or anything stand in your way.''

Jessie thought of Dan. She wanted to tell Merle about his threat. She wished she could ask him for advice, but even though he had come into her life and she was thankful for it, she still didn't know him—not enough to make him her confidante. And with that old ingrained teaching to stand on her own two feet whispering inside her, she couldn't bring herself to say the words.

''I'm going to try,'' she said, offering him a shaky smile. Then, forcing a cheerfulness she was far from feeling to her voice, she asked, ''What about you? How long are you going to stay?''

Merle shook his head. ''I'm not sure. I'd like to see your mother and try to at least come to some sort of understanding, but from what you say it would be a waste of time.''

''Probably,'' Jessie murmured.

''I would like to see a bit more of you and Cissy while I'm here.''

''That's no problem.''

''I know. Thank you.'' They sat in a companionable silence for a few minutes, and then Merle said, ''Tell me more about your dream.''

Jessie's laughter sounded stilted, embarrassed. She swirled the lemonade around in her glass. "It was pretty farfetched, really. I wanted everyone in the racing world to know who Jessie Harper was. I wanted to have some good horses. Maybe a really big horse." She gave Merle a quick, embarrassed look. "Pretty silly, huh?"

His smile was indulgent. "Silly, no. Ambitious, yes. But then, what else could I expect from Vera's daughter?"

Jessie laughed. Merle joined her. Sunshine poured down from a clear, azure sky on an aging man and a woman in her prime, each sorry for all the wasted years, but thankful that they'd found one another at last.

"I caught one, Bodie!" Cissy's voice shrilled in excitement.

The announcement brought Jessie from her prone position on the upper level of the boat where she'd been sunning while Bodie and Cissy fished and Merle rested. Rising, she moved to the rail where she could look down and see what was going on.

"Okay, honey. Start reeling it in real slow and careful," Bodie said, moving toward her. "That's it."

Jessie watched him sidle down the narrow walkway that surrounded the cabin of the boat, her heart scampering to keep up with her breathing at the arresting picture he made in his faded and frayed cutoffs, which left his muscular legs and the magnificent expanse of his chest bare. The pelt of curling hair covered his chest and trickled down his lean, muscled stomach, inviting exploration beyond the barrier of denim that rode low on his hips. Desire coiled in the pit of Jessie's femininity, and she had to force her mind back to the scene being played out before her.

Cissy had reeled the fish near the side even though it struggled against the line. "Wow!" Bodie exclaimed as he neared the child. "That's a keeper!"

The child beamed and continued to reel in the fighting fish. Her face was red from sun and effort, and Jessie smiled when she saw Cissy's tongue peek out the side of her mouth in a familiar gesture as she zeroed all her concentration in on landing the creature.

"Need any help?" Bodie asked when it became apparent that she was getting tired.

"No. I can do it," the child said with a determination that was achingly familiar. Her avowal to do it alone was so much like Jessie that Bodie felt a shaft of pain pierce his heart.

The fish splashed harder; Cissy's face grew redder.

"It's okay to get help if you need it, Cissy," he said soothingly. "Some things we just can't do by ourselves."

"I can..." Her hand slipped, halting her words and bringing a gasp of shock to her face as the fish made a bid for freedom and the reel began to hum as the line went skimming back out. "Bodie!" she cried, turning to him.

He was beside her in a second, stooping behind her and curling his big hands over hers on the rod. He locked the reel, then began a slow, steady cranking. Cissy put her hand on his as he turned the handle. She leaned back against him and, taking turns doing the reeling, they carefully brought the fish in.

"I'll get the net, honey. You hang on to him. Okay?" Bodie hoped she had the strength to keep the fish from escaping a second time, but knew it was important for her to feel she had done most of the work. She nodded and he rose and went to the front of the boat where the fishing supplies were kept in a locker, returning in a matter of seconds and bending to scoop the fish safely into the net.

"We did it!" Cissy cried, flinging her arms around his bare legs. She tilted her face back to look up at him, wearing an ear-to-ear smile.

Bodie reached and cradled her chin in the cup of his fingers. His own face held a quiet triumph. "That we did, honey."

He squatted down and pulled her against his bare chest, pressing a kiss to her freckled, sun-blushed cheek, the fish forgotten in the new closeness bonding them.

Jessie felt a lump forming at the base of her throat. To fight the incipient tears, she called down, "Way to go, gang!"

Bodie and Cissy looked up, smiles wreathing both their faces. "Can I go show Grandpa?" Cissy asked.

"Sure thing!" Jessie called, her happiness bringing a lilt to her voice. "He's sleeping the afternoon away! Go tell him to get up before the sun warps his ribs."

"Okay!" Cissy broke free of Bodie and scampered to the door of the cabin.

Bodie looked up at Jessie standing at the railing. "You stay put," he commanded in a curiously husky voice. "I'm coming up as soon as I get this fish on a stringer."

Jessie gave him a jaunty salute and said crisply, "Aye aye, cap'n."

He came up the steps in just a few moments. Jessie lay on her stomach, her chin propped in her hand, watching his approach. When he sat down beside her, she rolled to her side and said, "You're disgustingly sexy, Lattimer. You know that?"

He smiled lopsidedly. "You mean for an old man of forty?"

"Forty, my love, is definitely not old. It's mature."

"Hmm," he said, cocking his head to one side in a considering manner. "Mature. So that's why you find me irresistible."

Jessie didn't miss the twinkle of mischief in his eyes. She tilted her head, miming his attitude. "Hmm. The maturity, definitely. But then again, it could be your body that drives me crazy. What do you think?"

Bodie put his hand on the back of her neck and pulled her closer. He dropped a light kiss to her lips and said, "I think I'd like to explore the part where you called me your love. Am I?"

Jessie's brows lifted and her head canted to the side in contemplation. She pursed her lips. "Hmm... Must have been a slip of the tongue."

"A slip of the tongue?"

"Yeah."

A look that could only be classified as naughty crept into his green eyes and his hand moved in slow deliberation to the tie of her bikini top, which nestled between her breasts. "I'll show you a slip of the tongue."

His meaning was obvious. She caught his hand with hers. "You can't do that up here. Are you crazy?" she said in a near whisper.

"Uh-huh," he murmured, leaning over and pressing his lips to her sun-warmed shoulder while his hand worked free of her hold. "About you."

The fabric fell away and her breasts were exposed to the heat of the sunlight and his gaze. His rough fingers cupped one rounded globe, lifting and caressing with a gentleness that stole her thoughts while his mouth moved up the slender column of her neck, across the line of her jaw and to the corner of her mouth.

"Bodie..." she groaned, just before his mouth took hers. "What about Merle and Cissy?"

"Merle won't come up here, and you told Cissy she couldn't."

"But . . ."

"Shut up, Jessie," he whispered against her lips, "and kiss me."

The longing in his voice was her undoing. Jessie's eyes drifted closed and her mouth sought his blindly, her hands winnowing through the thickness of his hair. Bodie feasted on her mouth, nibbling, kissing, drawing her bottom lip into his mouth with a gentle suckling that drove her mindless with wanting. The boat rocked gently and off in the distance an airplane droned, but neither noticed.

When Bodie transferred his attention from her lips to her breasts, curling his tongue around first one turgid nipple and then the other, Jessie thought she would go completely crazy. She arched closer to him and felt the proof of his arousal pressing against her as the sound of the plane grew nearer. Part of her chanted that what she was doing was madness; the other part of her said, "So what?"

Suddenly, the droning of the plane's engine was transposed into a full-fledged roar as it neared the boat. Jessie was hurtled back to the reality of the moment, and Bodie's head lifted. He turned and looked up just in time to see the small single-engine aircraft pass over them. Jessie heard him mumble an irritated "damn" before he leaned over her, shielding her from the pilot's view. She was thankful for small favors, because the plane was so low she could actually see the pilot's grinning face as he passed by.

The moment that had seemed so right, so special only seconds before, now seemed cheap, tawdry. Guilt swamped her. And Dan's threat whirled through her mind with a vengeance. Jessie pushed Bodie away and struggled to retie her top. "I told you this was a crazy idea," she muttered, fumbling with the strings.

Puzzled by the completeness of her withdrawal and the near frenzy of her actions, Bodie captured her hands and forced her face up. Looking deeply into her eyes, he said, "Settle down, sweetheart. It might have been a crazy idea, but what happened wasn't so earth-shattering, was it?"

Jessie drew in a deep breath, reason and sanity returning in slow degrees. "Normally, I'd agree with you. But when I saw that man looking down at us, I couldn't help but think of Dan."

"Dan? What are you talking about?"

"What if Dan has hired detectives?"

"Jessie..."

"What if that pilot was hired to check..."

Once again, Bodie's hand went behind her head and he silenced her with a kiss. When he drew back, she had tears in her eyes. "You're getting paranoid, Jessie."

A tear slipped free and tumbled down her cheek. "I know. I can't help it. Vera said that since we are sleeping together it will make things worse."

Bodie nudged her hands aside and tied the strings of her top. When his eyes met hers, they were bland, emotionless. "If you're this upset, maybe we should just forget about us until everything blows over."

"No!" She shook her head and more tears followed the first. "No. I've waited too long for you. I can't give you up now."

Her announcement surprised him. Somehow, he'd thought he might come out a loser again. Bodie cradled one of her hands in his. "You don't have to give me up. We can still be together, but maybe we should keep things platonic until we know this is settled."

Jessie swiped at her tears. "You'd do that?"

He smiled. "I won't like it, but I'm fairly civilized, and I think I can handle it for a while."

Jessie could hardly believe what she heard. Thankfulness swept through her like a healing balm. Leaning nearer, she murmured, "I always knew there was some reason I loved you, Bodie Lattimer."

He smiled and took her lips, praying that he was doing the right thing. Praying that he wouldn't lose her again.

Miles away, Vera Harper sat on the edge of her bed, staring down at a picture in her lap. Two faces smiled happily up at her. The woman was dark and pretty and wore a white wedding gown. The man was blond, dashing and debonair in his black tuxedo. They were young and in love, unaware of the stresses the world would force on their fledgling feelings.

Vera traced the man's face with her fingertip, then pressed her finger to her lips. A single tear splashed onto the surface of glass before she drew herself upright and resolutely put the picture back in the box where it had been for so many years. Out of sight, but never out of mind.

Chapter Nine

Later that night, Bodie tossed restlessly, finally reaching for a cigarette in a desperate attempt to stay his thoughts. He couldn't forget the look on Jessie's face when she'd pulled away from him. She was having second thoughts and that scared him to death. He understood how upset she was over Dan's threat, but it was, after all, just that—a threat.

He frowned in the darkness. What kind of man would threaten to take a child away from a mother who appeared to be very good at her job? Oh, he understood that thinking your ex-wife was sleeping with someone else might rattle your cage a little, especially if you still cared for her, but from what Jessie said, there was little love lost between herself and Dan.

So what was it? Was Dan Givens so perfect he'd stayed lily-pure from the time he and Jessie divorced until he married Francine? Blowing a stream of smoke toward the ceiling, he smiled at the night. Doubtful. Or was it simply that Dan wanted to hurt Jessie the way she had hurt him? From the little he'd seen of her former husband, this prospect seemed more likely.

Where would it all end? Would Jessie wind up with Cissy, or would Dan use this new hold he had over Jessie to make her jump to his tune? And would Bodie Lattimer still be in the picture when it was all over? Surely after waiting for Jessie so long, God wouldn't be so cruel as to take her away from him again. But if Dan really did mean business and Jessie lost Cissy, it would be incredibly easy to lay the blame at his feet. He stubbed out his half-smoked cigarette and plumped his battered pillow again.

It all boiled down to one thing: how much did Jessie really love him?

By Friday, Jessie had worked herself into a state. Merle was going back to Florida the next afternoon, and he and Bodie were playing with Cissy in the living room while Jessie paced. Francine had called to say she would come for Cissy as usual. Jessie expected that. She only wondered if Francine would bring Cissy back. Vera's continuing assurances that they had to bring the child home until a judge decided otherwise hadn't gone very far in calming Jessie's fears.

Cissy played on, unaware that she was the cause of so much inner unrest. Merle glanced up from the game a few times to give his daughter a strange look, but Jessie was so nervous she didn't notice. Bodie, who saw Merle's concern, knew he was wondering what was wrong with her. He also knew that Jessie hadn't told him anything about Dan's threat and that Merle was most likely chalking up her sudden case of nerves to the fact that there was bad blood between Jessie and Dan's new wife.

When Francine's knock finally sounded at the door, Jessie's pacing stopped. Her gaze flew toward the sound, moved to Bodie and back to the door again. Like a sleepwalker, she moved forward, her shaking legs barely supporting her. She turned the knob and, thankful for the support, swung the door open to reveal Francine, whose smile looked as shaky as Jessie's legs felt.

"Hi. Is Cissy ready?"

"Yes. Come on in, and I'll get her things." Jessie knew her voice sounded defensive, and she hated herself for it. She wondered where the camaraderie she and Francine had once been reaching toward had gone. Stifling an inner panic, she stepped aside to let the other woman in.

Bodie watched as Francine entered the room. He stifled a smile at the surprise on her face when she saw him sitting on the floor playing with Cissy. He imagined that the last thing she expected was to find was him sitting in Jessie's living room after Dan's accusation and threat. Francine stood uncomfortably near the door until Cissy saved the moment by leaping up and running to give her a hug. Merle pushed to his feet for an introduction and Bodie sat and waited to see what would happen next.

In spite of her agitation, the manners Vera had instilled came to Jessie's aid. "Merle, this is Dan's wife, Francine. Francine, this is my father, Merle Harper."

Merle offered Francine a smile and his hand simultaneously. "Hello. I see you get the little beastie for the weekend." He looked down at Cissy and tweaked one braid. "Well, good riddance, I say!"

Francine's gaze flicked to Jessie then slid to Bodie a second before she replied, "Yes."

Cissy, grown used to his teasing, tugged on her grandfather's slacks and giggled. "Grandpa!"

"Well, good luck with her! By the way, do you know Bodie?" Merle asked, a gleam of laughter still in his eyes.

Francine nodded, her eyes moving hesitantly from Merle to Bodie. "We've . . . met."

One corner of Bodie's mustache crawled upward in a sardonic smile and he winked at Francine with an audaciousness that took Jessie's breath away. "How's it goin', Francine?"

Her eyes widened in surprise and she licked her lips. "I'm fine, thank you." Then in a rush, she said, "Are you ready, Cissy?"

"Yes, ma'am."

Cissy kissed each adult in turn, including Bodie, who held her tightly and said, "Be good, tiger."

She grinned at him and crossed her heart. "Promise." Then she picked up her overnight case with both hands and started for the door.

Jessie stood twisting her hands in spite of herself. "I guess I'll see you Sunday evening."

No one could miss the pain and wistfulness that was mirrored in her dark eyes. Not even Francine. An empathetic pain swept through Bodie. He hated seeing Jessie so vulnerable.

"Yes," she said breathlessly. "We'll see you Sunday night." Her need to escape was obvious as she shepherded Cissy toward the door.

As Cissy, Merle and Jessie chorused their goodbyes, Bodie sat staring at the closing door, wondering if he had only imagined the compassion he heard in Francine's voice.

When the door shut behind them, Merle said, "She seems nice enough."

"Yes. She is," Jessie said, meaning every word. "She's good to Cissy."

"Francine's all right," Bodie agreed, rising and going to slide an arm around Jessie's shoulders.

"Well, kids," Merle said, with a friendly thump on Bodie's shoulder, "I hate to run, but I have some packing to do, and I think I'll get a good night's rest before the trip tomorrow."

"That would probably be a good idea," Jessie agreed. "You look tired. Are you sure you're feeling okay?"

Merle smiled. Only Bodie, who had seen him take a pill earlier, noticed that his cheerfulness was forced. "I'm as good as can be expected at my age, so don't go worrying about me."

"Okay. I won't. Is there anything I can do to help you get ready?"

"Not that I know of." He kissed Jessie's cheek. "I'll see you tomorrow afternoon before I leave."

She nodded, fighting the ache of tears gathering in her throat. She watched Merle and Bodie shake hands and then her father was out the door, striding to his car in the shadows of early evening.

She closed the door and stood leaning against it, sadness etched on her features. "I hate to see him go," she confessed.

Bodie nodded. "I know. But you'll be able to see him again soon. He'll be back."

She sighed and pushed from the door, going straight into his arms. "I know. But it doesn't make it any easier to say goodbye."

"It never does." He held her and rocked from side to side, offering her what comfort he could in the face of the losses threatening her. Finally, he kissed the top of her head and murmured, "You okay now?"

Jessie leaned back and looked up at him, love shining from her eyes. "I'm okay."

"Good. I didn't want to leave you all torn up."

"Leave. Why?"

He lifted his eyebrows in disbelief. "Our agreement. Remember? Our platonic relationship?"

Jessie thrust out her bottom lip in a pout that resembled Cissy's. "I remember. But I don't like it."

He slid his hands into the back pockets of her jeans and pulled her flush against his hard maleness. "Do you think I do?" he growled, before he lowered his mouth to hers in a bruising, hungry kiss.

Breathless moments later, he lifted his head. His hands shook as he drew them from her pockets and rested them on her shoulders to set her from him. "I've got to get out of here while I still can," he said in a hoarse voice.

Jessie's smile was both wistful and sexy. "You've got to get out of here while I'll still let you."

Bodie laughed softly and kissed her again before he let himself out, promising he'd stop by when he finished at the track the next day.

Once he had gone, silence and loneliness settled into the trailer with a vengeance. Jessie rattled around, doing nothing, finally deciding that eating would take up some time and fixing herself a sandwich. Then she sat in front of a television show she had no interest in and wondered how—and with whom—Bodie was spending his Friday night since they couldn't spend it in one another's arms. She wondered if Merle had his packing done and if he truly felt all right. And she wondered if Dan was filling Cissy's malleable mind with his uncharitable opinions of her mother.

She dropped the sandwich to the plate and set it on the coffee table. Rising, she went to the window, pushed back the sheer curtain and stared out into the encroaching evening. Should she call Bodie? They could talk on the phone, couldn't they? Or would Dan see that as unfit behavior?

She let the curtain fall and, with frustration marring every move, began to clean up the minimal mess she'd created fixing her sandwich. It was the waiting, she thought as she put her dirty plate into the dishwasher. The waiting and wondering what Dan would do—if anything. Could his threat be just that—something to keep her where he wanted her? A way to guarantee that he could manipulate his relationship with Cissy to his own advantage?

No. She didn't think so. Dan was thorough and meticulous in his dealings. He didn't promise what he couldn't deliver. New panic flooded her at the thought. She tossed the dishcloth into the draining water, staring at it and gripping the edge of the sink with white-knuckled intensity.

Damn it, Dan! Do something!

Something concrete—anything—would be better than this. Something tangible could be dealt with in some way, but this...

A sharp knocking brought her head up and around. She'd longed for companionship to get her through the long night, but now that someone was here, all she wanted was to be left alone. Drawing in a deep breath to steady her rocky nerves, she wiped her damp hands on the sides of her jeans and went to answer the door.

Vera stood there, dressed in her usual jeans and shirt, a look on her face that was easily recognizable to Jessie. It was the same one she wore. Loneliness. The two women stood, just looking at one another and, for the first time Jessie could remember, she didn't feel on edge in her mother's presence, didn't feel resentment gnawing at her.

She forced a smile and moved back. "Hi. Come on in, Mother."

Vera stepped over the threshold. "Were you busy? I was just... killing time."

Jessie shook her head and laughed shortly. "No. I wasn't busy. I was just sitting here feeling sorry for myself. What about you? I thought you had a dinner date with Frank Jeffries."

"I did," Vera said, putting her purse on an end table. "I cancelled it."

"Why?"

Vera shrugged. "I'm beginning to think I did it for the reasons you told me. Because I sense that he wants more than I want to give him."

"A roll in the hay?" Jessie asked, sinking into a comfortable arm chair.

Vera plopped onto the worn sofa and shook her dark head. "Strangely enough, no." She looked up at Jessie with an almost embarrassed look. "I think the man is looking for a wife."

"You?"

Vera shrugged. "Who knows? I was talking to Jimmie Rae the other day and she seems to think that since his first marriage was so great, he's anxious to marry again, even though his wife hasn't been dead all that long."

"That makes sense to me," Jessie said.

Vera looked surprised. "It does?"

"Sure. He wants to find that happiness again."

"Well," Vera said, "he sure wouldn't find it with me."

"Are you so sure of that?"

A smile curved the older woman's lips. "Is this the same daughter talking to me who thinks I'm such an ogre?"

Jessie smiled back. "Not an ogre, Mother. Just stubborn and extremely," she drawled, "opinionated."

"I am that," Vera said with a sigh. "I can't imagine why he would want to court me. Everyone on the backside knows I never date one man long."

"He's after your body," Jessie quipped, interested in this new, more human Vera. At least Vera's problems put her own on hold momentarily. She curled her legs up under her and leaned forward. "So tell me," she urged. "What's he like?"

The next quarter hour was spent in girl talk. Jessie didn't ever recall her mother being so open about her feelings or her fears. And she couldn't remember ever caring one way or the other how her mother felt.

They were laughing over Vera's embarrassment when Frank had taken her to meet his grown children when another knock sounded at the door. Laughing, Jessie bounded from the chair and swept a loose tendril of hair out of her eyes. She threw open the door, her face still wreathed with a smile, but the smile and the pleasure she felt vanished in an instant when she saw who was standing in the doorway. All the blood drained from her face, then rushed back with a force that made her dizzy.

The man, dressed in sympathy and the brown uniform of the sheriff's department, lifted his brows and asked, "Jessica Harper?"

Jessie could only nod and grip the doorknob...and wait for the words that would destroy her world.

Vera, whose heart stopped beating when she saw who was at the door, felt that same heart plunge to the pit of her soul when she saw the deputy hold out an official-looking document.

Jessie reached for the papers automatically, staring down at them with a horror that was reflected back in her soft brown eyes.

"I'm sorry," the man said, before turning and retracing his steps to the car.

Mutely, Jessie watched him go. Then she turned back to the living room and closed the door, leaning against it because she wasn't certain her legs could hold her up. She stared across the room, unaware of

Vera's presence. The paper burned her fingers. Without looking, she knew the waiting was over. She now had something tangible to fight. She knew it as certainly as she knew the sun would set in the west the following day.

She began to unfold the paper with hands that shook so badly it was hard to read the typewritten words. Or did her inability to read stem from the fact that the tears she hadn't shed for so long had defied her mind's wishes and were flooding her eyes and trickling down her cheeks with ever increasing speed? Regardless of her tears and blurred vision the message on the paper was as clear as the crystal-like droplets that fell onto its surface.

Dan had kept his promise. He was suing for custody of Cissy.

Her keening wail broke the silence as well as the spell of immobility holding Vera in its grip. She sprang up and crossed to where Jessie stood, a trembling mass of hurting humanity who was tied to Vera's heartstrings by the strongest bond on earth. Blood.

Wrapping her arms around her daughter, she held Jessie close, rocking her in much the same way Bodie had earlier, much the way she had rocked her when she had been hurt as a child. But Jessie wasn't a child any longer. She was a grown woman with a grown woman's problems. And this time, Vera knew she couldn't kiss it and make it better. All she could do was hold her, hurt with her and pray for miracles she no longer believed in.

If Jessie had thought the evening loomed ahead of her, it was nothing compared to the actual length of the night. When her tears dried and she felt as empty as the twice-drained coffeepot, she and Vera had talked. And talked. About Dan. About Merle. About Bodie. And eventually, Cissy. Lifelong problems, decade-old myths and ancient misunderstandings had been dragged from the corners of their hearts and examined in minutest detail.

It had been a long night. A grueling night. But when they fell into an exhausted sleep shortly before it was time to get up and go to the track, each felt as if the slate between them had been wiped clean of past misdeeds and mistakes. And when the alarm had summoned them from their troubled dreams, each woke with a new determination to be better to themselves and others—especially to those they loved.

Jessie worked throughout the morning, alternately despondent and lighthearted, depending on whether her thoughts centered on Cissy or Vera. Vera had left the track early, without saying where she was going. Jessie was raking the shedrow when Merle arrived to say goodbye and the realization that he was leaving struck her.

Fresh sadness engulfed her. It wasn't enough to worry about Dan's intent and wonder how best to deal with it—now she had to say goodbye to a father she'd just met. It was more than she thought she could bear.

"I came to take you to lunch, but you look awfully busy," Merle said with a smile, sitting on a bale of hay and mopping at his perspiring forehead with a pristine white hanky.

"Almost finished," Jessie told him, raking with a vengeance.

"Hey! Slow down!" he said with a laugh. "It's too hot to be going at that like you're killing snakes."

Relenting, she stopped, leaned on the rake handle and sighed. "You're right. It is."

Merle saw the dark circles beneath her eyes and the pallor undermining her tan. "Excuse me for being so ungentlemanly as to say so, but you look like hell, Jessie."

Her startled eyes flew to his. He'd noticed. *As if anyone could help it!* She didn't want him to know about Dan and Cissy. She still wasn't certain their new and tentative relationship could stand the burden. Besides, he looked as tired as she felt. *So lighten up, Jessie. Don't let on.*

Her smile was as fake as the diamond Cissy got out of the gum machine a few days before. "It's just that I hate to see you go."

Her confession wiped the smile from his lips. "I know. I hate leaving you and Cissy, too. But it won't be twenty-seven years before I see you next time."

"Promise?" she asked with a half-smile.

"Promise."

Merle and Jessie ate a leisurely lunch at the Ramada Inn in Bossier City. She did her utmost to keep the conversation on light, positive subjects. She tried her hardest to push Dan, the custody suit and Merle's leaving to the back of her mind. And it seemed to work—at least until he dropped her off at the track and they said their final farewells.

Jessie didn't know how it happened. One minute they were discussing their next meeting, the next she was in her father's arms for the first time in more than a score of years. She wasn't certain how long he held her, but when she pulled away, there were tears in Merle's eyes, too.

Jessie had just finished her shower and was pulling on a pair of shorts when Bodie arrived. Her heart was heavy when she opened the door to him, and that sorrow must have bled through the smile she gave him.

"What's the matter, sweetheart?" he asked, pulling her into a comforting embrace and kissing the top of her head.

Jessie held him tightly, fighting the tears that sought escape. She shook her head against his chest. "Just hold me."

He did. Calmness came with the steady beating of his heart and the way his hands moved over her— softly, sweetly and without any hint of sexuality. Finally, she lifted her head to look at him. "Thank you."

He knew without words what she was talking about. "Any time." He paused a second and asked, "Has Merle gone?"

"No." She glanced at the clock. "He should be leaving any time now."

"Is that why you're so upset?"

Jessie pulled from his loose grasp. "That's part of it." Moving toward the sofa, she cast him a look over her shoulder and asked, "Have you seen Vera?"

Frowning, he followed. "Vera? No. Why?"

"I thought she might have told you about last night."

"Jessie!" Bodie exclaimed, drawing the wrong conclusion. "You didn't fight with your mother again, did you?"

Sinking down into the corner of the sofa, she said, "No. As a matter of fact, you'll be proud to know that my mother and I have settled all our old problems."

Bodie sat down beside her. "Yeah? What happened? Did you have Judge Wapner come and sit in while you argued it out?" he asked facetiously.

In spite of her heavy heart, Jessie flashed him a withering look. "Cute, Lattimer."

"Thanks," he responded in kind.

Jessie sobered and took his hand in both of hers, rubbing the dark hair on the back with one fingertip. "I had an unexpected visitor last night."

Bodie's brows lifted in question.

"Someone from the sheriff's department." Bodie's curse was drowned out by her voice as she continued. "He served me with papers on the custody suit. I have to appear in court in three weeks."

"I can't believe this. I never really thought he would go this far. What's the matter with the idiot, anyway?"

"I guess he thinks he's in the right."

Anger settled on Bodie's face like a dark thundercloud. "I guess maybe I could go and set his thinking straight."

His meaning wasn't lost on Jessie. Her grip on his hand tightened. "No, Bodie. Fighting won't help."

"Maybe not," he said darkly, "but I'd sure as hell feel better."

A picture of Bodie and Dan dancing around one another, fists raised, flashed through Jessie's mind. She began to laugh softly. It was ludicrous. The whole thing was ludicrous.

"What's so funny?" Bodie asked.

Jessie didn't answer. She only laughed harder. She had to laugh or she might start crying again. And even though she'd cried until there were no more tears left, she knew that if she ever started, she might not be able to stop.

Merle was almost ready to call a taxi when he heard the timid knocking at his motel-room door. Clicking the catches of his suitcase shut and wondering who it could be, he moved toward the door. A woman stood there. Older, yes, but just as slim and attractive as she'd ever been—even with the white streak through her dark hair. Still, if Jessie hadn't told him, he wasn't certain he would have known who she was. He was so engrossed with his examination that the fact that she was looking him over just as carefully never registered.

"Merle?" she asked, speaking at last.

He couldn't help but smile. Even if he hadn't recognized her, he would have recognized her voice anywhere. Vera had changed in many ways, but her husky whiskey-and-cigarettes voice hadn't.

"Hello, Vee," he said, lapsing without thought into the nickname he'd once called her and trying not to show his surprise at her unexpected appearance. "Come in."

Clutching the purse she was carrying, she stepped through the door, looking around the tastefully appointed room with interest. "Nice room," she commented inanely.

"Yes, it is," Merle agreed. He swept a shaving case from a chair and offered, "Have a seat."

She sat down on the edge of the striped chair and gripped her purse with both hands.

"Would you like something to drink? There's a soda machine outside."

"No, thank you," she demurred, not quite meeting his eyes.

Merle sat down on the room's other chair, crossed his legs and studied his former wife's face. "You're looking great, Vera."

Vera turned toward him; their eyes met squarely. So many years between them. So many feelings—good and bad. Love. Disappointment. Hate. And a child. A child who needed them both.

He's changed. This is a stronger Merle Harper than I knew. It was there in the way his eyes met hers—with a directness and confidence lacking before. The old Merle had worn three-piece suits to project an aura of authority. Now that authority was apparent by the set of his shoulders and the casual negligence in the way he wore his clothes. Still, though there was a new confidence in him, Vera noticed that he was too thin and pale. There was something else, too. A sadness. A weariness that went beyond the physical. It was a sadness of the soul.

"Thank you," she said at last. "You look good, too. A little thin, maybe."

Merle shrugged and smiled—a shadow of the smile that had captured her heart more than thirty years before. "Too much restaurant cooking."

He crossed one ankle over his knee and grasped the ankle with his hand, waiting for Vera to expound on her reason for coming.

"Jessie has really enjoyed the time you've spent with her," she said after a few seconds of silence, her words serving as more of an icebreaker than anything else.

Merle smiled. "I've enjoyed being with her and Cissy, too." There was a hint of sadness in his eyes when he added, "I'm only sorry I didn't come sooner."

Before Vera could monitor her speech or wonder where her question would lead, she asked, "Why didn't you? She's needed you so many times through the years."

"Because you told me not to come back, remember?" he reminded her.

Yes, she remembered. The screamed threats about what she would do if he dared try to see them again rushed back with a vengeance. "Yes. I remember." She held his gaze steadily. "I was wrong to keep you apart."

"I know that now. And I was wrong for not coming anyway," he told her, unwilling that she shoulder all the blame. "We were both wrong, Vera, and we can't change that. All we can do is go on from here. I can't make up to Jessie for all those years, but I can be here for her in the future."

"I know," Vera said. "That's why I'm here."

Merle's brows drew together in a frown. "What do you mean?"

"I mean that you shouldn't leave now. Jessie needs you."

He uncrossed his legs and leaned toward her. "Why? What's happened? Is Cissy all right? Is it money?'' He fired the questions off in rapid succession.

Vera held up a silencing hand. "Cissy is all right—physically. So is Jessie. But she's having a problem with Dan.''

Merle frowned and rested his elbows on his knees. "What kind of problem?''

"To make a long story short, Francine brought Cissy home one day, and when Jessie sent her into her bedroom to put away a gift she'd bought her, Cissy found Bodie in her mother's bed.''

Merle's distress was obvious from the sudden paleness of his face. "And Dan is making a big thing out of it?''

Vera's lips twisted. "You might say that. He's suing for custody of her.''

"Damn!'' Merle rose and drew his hand down his face in a gesture that betrayed his agitation.

Vera watched him pace the room and tried to explain. "Bodie had been drinking and fighting. He came to Jessie for some conversation and sympathy. She let him sleep it off on the sofa. After she got up and went to work, he got in her bed. Nothing happened.''

"That time,'' Merle supplied correctly, knowing there was more to Bodie and Jessie's relationship.

"Yes,'' Vera said with a sigh. "They're trying to stay away from one another as much as possible because Jessie knows it will hurt her position if Dan's accusations are true.''

"That's smart. I doubt if anything will come of it if Jessie plays it cool.''

"You don't understand, Merle. Dan doesn't make idle threats. He's somewhat of a perfectionist and expects everyone else to be, too. He's already had the papers served."

"What!" Merle exploded. "How in hell did he get anything done so fast?"

"He has money. And he has a lot of friends in high places."

Merle sank onto the edge of the bed and his right hand came up and began an automatic massaging of his left arm. If possible he grew even more pale.

"Merle..." Vera said, half-rising when she saw the grimace that contorted his features for a split second. "Are you all right?"

He indicated the shaving kit with one hand. "There's a bottle of pills there. Would you get me one, please?"

Vera was already reaching for the leather case. She flashed him an accusing look even as she rummaged around in the case. "It's your heart, isn't it?"

He nodded.

Vera spied the pills and, uncapping the bottle, shook one out and rushed it to him. Merle popped the pill into his mouth and under his tongue, then closed his eyes and eased back against the headboard, waiting for it to work.

Vera sat beside him on the bed's edge, holding his hand, feeling for his rapid pulse and praying that he would be all right. In a matter of minutes the color returned to his face and his breathing became easier, less labored. The pulse galloping beneath her fingertips slowed. Merle's eyes fluttered open and he looked at her with something close to an apology gleaming from their depths.

"Is it bad?" she asked, concern pleating her brow.

"Bad enough," he replied with an attempted smile.

Comprehension dawned slowly. It all made sense now. Merle was playing his heart condition down, but instinct told Vera that it was worse than he let on. His heart was bad enough that he was trying to mend his fences.

What was it about age, anyway? Was it that the years piling up made you more aware of your mortality? Was that why Merle wanted to set things straight? And was that why she'd come to him for help? She'd told herself that it was for Jessie—because Jessie needed him. But was it? Really?

"Why didn't you tell someone?"

"Who?" he countered with a wistful smile. "You, my divorced wife? Jessie—the child I didn't even know?"

Shock held Vera silent. She looked deeply into the soft brown eyes she'd once been able to drown in. "Surely," she said at last, "there's someone?"

Merle's head moved side to side in a negative motion. "No. No one. If you'll remember, I married again soon after we split up. It lasted a year...less, actually." He closed his eyes and sighed. "After you left me, I think I did some changing. I knew I'd been wrong. I knew I should have been stronger—tried harder to make things work. But the second time around, it just didn't seem worth the effort." His eyes locked with hers. "Maybe she wasn't worth the effort."

Vera watched as his eyes closed again, as if he feared she might see too much revealed there. "I'm sorry," she told him in genuine sympathy, reminded of her own lonely life.

Behind his closed eyelids, a silent montage of memories played on the backdrop of his mind. Vera at twenty—happy, bubbly, vivacious...and loving. His mouth curved in a slight, sorrowful smile. "So am I, Vee. So am I."

Chapter Ten

In spite of all Jessie's worrying, Francine brought Cissy home on Sunday evening just as she'd said she would. Jessie didn't know if it was her imagination or if there really was a new compassion in the younger woman's eyes when they met hers across the threshold.

"She was an angel," Francine told her, tucking a dark strand of hair behind her ear. "We took her to the Strand to see the ballet, and she couldn't have been better."

Jessie bristled with maternal pride. She tossed Cissy a grateful smile before giving Francine her thanks.

"You should have seen them, Mom!" Cissy exclaimed excitedly. "They wore fluffy skirts and—" she stood up as tall as she could on her tennis-shoe-clad toes "—walked on their toes." Lifting her arms, she began to show them her own style of *port de bras*.

Jessie and Francine laughed, forgetting the tension between them for a moment. "She's a ham," Francine said.

"Yes, she is."

As suddenly and without warning as it had left, the constraint returned, erasing the smiles from both their faces. "Well, I'd best be going," Francine said at last.

She turned to leave and all of a sudden Jessie could stand the game playing no longer. "Wait!"

At the bottom of the steps, Francine turned, her eyes questioning.

"We need to talk," Jessie said. At Francine's reluctant nod, Jessie turned to Cissy and said, "Go empty your suitcase, sugar."

They watched Cissy leave the room and, without a word, Francine retraced her steps and followed Jessie into the house. "Sit down," Jessie offered, sinking into her favorite corner of the sofa.

Francine settled into an armchair and crossed her shapely legs. Unease wiped the usual sparkle from her violet eyes.

Jessie cleared her throat. "There's no sense beating around the bush about what's on my mind. I'm sure you know Dan is suing for custody of Cissy."

Francine nodded.

"Because he thinks I slept with Bodie?"

"Yes."

"But I explained what happened to you. Did you tell him?"

"I tried...but you don't know how Dan is when he gets his teeth into something."

Jessie gave her companion a wan smile. "Don't I?" Francine nodded again. "Yeah. I guess you do."

Nervously, Jessie rose and strode across the room. "The strange thing is," she said with a hint of sarcasm, "I'm relatively sure Dan hasn't been celibate for the last five years."

She turned in time to see a betraying blush stain Francine's cheek. *Ah. So our all-American girl isn't perfect.* Jessie squashed the snide thought. Francine was human, after all, and her feelings for Cissy were genuine. Whatever was between her and Dan before their marriage—or after it, for that matter—was none of her business.

"Francine..."

The other woman looked up, embarrassment still hiding in her eyes.

"Why is he doing this? You probably know him better than I do, so why?"

Jessie saw the embarrassment in Francine's eyes make a subtle change to confusion. She knew something she wasn't telling.

"I love Dan. He's good to me. And good for me. I don't want anything to jeopardize that."

Jessie could relate to those same feelings with Bodie. She sat back down and faced Francine. "Neither do I, Francine. I have nothing against Dan, and I wish you both all the happiness in the world. Our marriage didn't work, and that was probably more my fault than his. I never really loved him the way I should have. At the time, I thought I did, but..."

"But you were in love with Bodie," Francine interjected.

Jessie frowned. "Yes. How did you know?"

"Whatever there is between the two of you is too strong to have been forged since he came back," Francine observed with a wisdom beyond her years.

"It shows?"

"Yes."

It was Jessie's turn to look embarrassed. She wondered how she had ever considered Francine superficial.

"Maybe I shouldn't say this, but . . ."

"But?" Jessie prompted.

"I think Dan is doing this to get back at you."

"Get back at me! For what?"

Francine's voice was thick with suppressed emotion. "Maybe for not loving him back."

Jessie's eyes widened in surprise. "Surely you aren't implying that he still cares for me?"

Francine shook her head, her dark hair swirling around her shoulders. "No. Not any more. I couldn't have married him if I didn't believe he loved me, but when I first met him he told me that some part of him still cared for his ex-wife. That's the reason we dated for more than a year. I had to be sure."

Jessie digested this new, surprising information. Of course she'd supposed Dan loved her when they married, and that had only served to fortify her guilt that she didn't love him back. But she'd never dreamed that he still felt anything for her so long after the divorce.

"You know," Francine said thoughtfully. "I was really jealous of you for a while."

"Jealous! Of me?" Jessie asked. "Why?"

"Because you're so together. So independent. So smart about what you do."

No one seeing the sincerity on Francine's face could doubt she meant it. Jessie began to laugh softly.

Francine watched her with a concerned look on her pretty face. "I don't get it," she said finally. "What's so funny about that?"

Jessie wiped her streaming eyes and tried to control her mirth. "Oh, Francine!" she gasped. "I've been jealous of you because you're exactly what Dan wanted in a wife. Someone totally domestic and content to let him be the center of her existence... something I wasn't."

Francine's mouth curved upward at the corners. "Silly, huh?"

"Yeah. Pretty silly," Jessie agreed.

They sat smiling over their confessions for a few seconds before Jessie finally spoke again. "I still don't understand why, if Dan cared for me and is happy with you now, he would deliberately try to hurt me."

"Pride," Francine said softly, again showing that wisdom Jessie hadn't thought she possessed. "That vulnerable male pride."

Pride. Jessie was familiar with pride... the spawn of hurt that kept you from showing your pain. The offspring of insecurity that kept your chin at an angle others called haughty, just so they couldn't read the vulnerability in your eyes. The thing that kept you working long, exhausting hours so others wouldn't look down on you for your lack of knowledge. The emotion that in one way or the other had separated her from the people she loved most...

But never again, she vowed silently. Never again.

After Francine left, Jessie called Bodie and told him about her conversation with Francine—especially about Dan's reason for continuing with the custody suit and her own feelings about Jessie.

He'd laughed about Francine's feelings, but had become quiet when she'd told him what Francine said about Dan wanting to get back at her for not loving him.

"Bodie? What's the matter?"

"Nothing," he said gruffly. She heard him sigh. "It's just that I know what he went through. I've been there."

Tears stung beneath Jessie's eyelids at the thought of her empty life the last few years and Bodie loving her and not knowing if that love would ever be returned. "I know," she whispered. "I'm sorry."

Silence crackled through the phone lines for a moment and then, with another sigh that seemed to empty him of all the sorrow, he asked, "Want to take Cissy and go to the Monroe Zoo tomorrow?"

"Believe me, I'd love to go, but if it won't make you mad I'd like to spend the day with Cissy alone."

"It won't make me mad. I understand."

The tears started again. "Do you?"

"Of course I do."

And somehow, hearing the tenderness and concern in his voice, she was positive that he did. "You'll come over when we get home tomorrow evening, won't you?"

"You bet."

The following morning, Jessie was still thinking of his answer. Though the time she spent with Cissy had always been special and important to her, how could Bodie know that it had taken on a new significance? Knowing she might lose the child made every moment they were together special. And that was why, when she finished at the track, she packed a picnic lunch and drove to the state-park pool for a day of fun and swimming—only to find the gates locked.

Undaunted by the fact that that area of the park was closed on Monday, they drove on down the road to the next spot. Though it didn't have a pool, there was a swimming area with a sandy beach. Picnic tables were situated beneath moss-festooned trees, easily within watching and shouting distance of the water.

They set out their picnic trappings, then Jessie stripped off her shorts and T-shirt to reveal a black one-piece suit splashed with brilliant tropical flowers. She twisted her long ponytail into a knot, securing it with several pins. Then she placed her hands on slender hips and taunted, "Bet you can't beat me to the water!"

"Bet I can!" Cissy quipped back over her shoulder, her feet in high gear before the words were out of her mouth. Then, as an added insult, she cried, "Last one in's a rotten egg!"

Jessie laughed and began to run toward the water's edge. Cissy hit the shallow water just seconds before her mother and stood laughing jubilantly because she'd won.

"Okay, Miss Priss," Jessie said haughtily. "Let's see how long you can hold your breath."

The next half hour was spent splashing, swimming and cavorting in the water. Then, spent and hungry, they trekked hand in hand back through the sand to the table, the water that ran off their sleek, water-spangled bodies, leaving two sets of wet footprints in the sand.

They feasted on sandwiches, potato chips and soda. Jessie watched Cissy's freckled gamine face as they talked and laughed and Cissy shared more of the special time she'd spent at the ballet.

"I like Francine," she said at last. "She's nice."

"Yes," Jessie agreed, "she is."

"And Daddy's nice, too, but he's been cross a lot lately," Cissy said.

"Oh?"

Cissy nodded and took a sip of her drink. "Him and Francine had a fight the other day," she confessed, taking a drink of her cola. Her blue eyes were filled with worry.

Jessie didn't know what to do. It was really none of her business, but she hated for Dan and Francine's problems to cause Cissy heartache. Before she could think of any way to circumvent hearing more about Dan's trouble with his wife, Cissy piped up again. "I think Daddy is mad at you and Bodie."

"Cissy. . . I don't think Daddy would want you to talk about his troubles to other people."

"But why is he mad at you, Mom?"

Damn you, Dan! "I don't know, sugar," she said, lying to Cissy for the first time in her life. Under the circumstances, it seemed the only acceptable thing to do. She drained her bottle and set it down with a thud. Forcing a happiness she was far from feeling, she said, "I bet I can build a better sand castle than you."

"Bet you can't!" Cissy replied saucily, her worry forgotten in the face of a new challenge.

Jessie romped with her daughter, storing the mental pictures of Cissy in a corner of her mind and heart where she could take them out and look at them . . . if and when the time ever came that she didn't have the original nearby.

They worked together for hours to build a giant sand castle. Jessie patted and shaped the wet sand and wondered what had been said about her and Bodie. Cissy worked along with her, her face serious and intent, her tongue peeking out of the corner of her mouth as they landscaped the castle with twigs, pebbles and wildflowers. They were both glowing with triumph when they finished their masterpiece and went back to the table to celebrate with a cold drink.

There was no warning when an older boy stopped to look at their handiwork and, in a malicious, premeditated gesture, swung his bare foot in a wide arc, sending the sand castle to its destruction in a shower of glistening silica.

Anger drew Cissy's face into rigid lines as she screamed at the boy to leave her sand castle alone. Crying, she begged Jessie to help her build it again; brokenhearted, Jessie maintained that rebuilding was an impossibility. Finally, unable to stand Cissy's tears any longer, Jessie went to her daughter and gathered her close. Picking her slight body up, she carried her to the table where she sat down on the bench and began to rock her. Murmuring in low tones, Jessie offered words of comfort and kissed each and every freckle adorning Cissy's face while the child cried against her breast until she fell asleep.

Thankful that her misery was temporarily at an end, Jessie leaned back against the table and held Cissy close, realizing that if Dan made good his threat, her life would be like the sand castle—ruined beyond rebuilding. Swallowing back the emotion clotting her throat, Jessie held Cissy close and watched the sunlight dappling her cheeks change as the sun dropped lower in the summer sky. She watched her and held her as other picnickers came and went—until her arms hurt from Cissy's slight weight and the pain became a blessed numbness. She watched until Cissy finally woke up two hours later.

And later, thinking back, she knew without a doubt that the picture she would always remember was one of Cissy asleep in her arms, her face flushed with heat, her hair in damp tendrils against her cheeks and her thumb in her mouth...something she'd done as a baby, but a security she hadn't felt the need of in more than three years.

While Jessie and Cissy were unpacking their picnic lunch at the lake, Bodie was treating Vera to lunch and listening to her tell of the visit she and Merle had made to Dan's house before Merle left on Sunday morning, instead of Saturday afternoon as planned.

"What made you decide to go to Merle for help?" Bodie asked as they sat down and began their lunch.

Vera speared a piece of lettuce. "Who better?" she challenged. "He's Jessie's father. And he has position and money. Why shouldn't he use it to help his own child?"

Bodie regarded the pooling juices of his steak for a moment, then said, "You're right. I guess it just surprised me that you would go to him."

Vera offered him a smile tinted with embarrassment. "To tell you the truth, it surprised me, too."

Bodie's eyes crinkled in a smile. "So how'd it go?"

"Surprisingly well. He's changed."

"Haven't we all?"

"Yes," Vera acknowledged with a sigh. She reached for her coffee. "You know, I've wished a hundred times things had been different."

"I imagine Merle has, too."

"Maybe." She brought the cup to her lips.

"I can see a definite change in you lately, Vera. Maybe now that the two of you have buried the hatchet, there's hope that you can forget the past and make something of the future."

Vera's laughter held a touch of wistfulness. "We've neither changed that much."

He shrugged. "You never know."

Setting the cup on the table, she captured his gaze. "He's a sick man, Bodie."

The news wasn't surprising. Not after Bodie had watched the older man's tired spells, his frequent resting and his furtive pill taking. "What is it?"

"His heart. Angina."

Bodie swore softly. "I'm glad he came back to meet Jessie."

"I'm glad he's come back for a lot of reasons, but especially because I don't feel that old hate gnawing at my insides the way I used to." She gave him a wan smile. "I wanted to hate him when I saw him, but I couldn't. I thought I'd see the man who'd taken my love and desecrated it by sharing it with other women—a man who killed that love because he didn't return it."

"And?" Bodie asked in a gentle voice.

"All I felt was sorry."

Knowing she was skirting the edge of an emotional precipice, Bodie shifted the conversational topic. "Do you think your visit to Dan was worth it?"

"I don't know. We tried. Merle was polite, but a bit abrasive. Dan didn't appear threatened, but then, you never know..."

"Maybe you gave him something to think about."

"We tried." She grew thoughtful a moment and when she finally looked at him, her eyes held unmistakable earnestness. "After everything our divorce has deprived Jessie of, going to Dan and standing up for her together about this seemed the very least we could do."

Bodie was silent, agreeing wholeheartedly and wondering, as he always did, why it was that children were always the victims of a separation—in one way or the other.

The phone was ringing when Jessie and Cissy entered the trailer. Cissy ran to get it while Jessie hefted the picnic basket to the cabinet top. Looking at the child from the corner of her eye, Jessie saw the wide smile that lit her face.

"Mom! It's Grandpa!"

Jessie felt a comparable smile forming as she went to the phone and waited for Cissy to finish telling Merle about their day at the lake. Jessie watched and felt a glow of happiness begin to edge aside the melancholy that had been her companion since Cissy had cried herself to sleep in her arms. When Cissy finally finished telling about her day, she handed the phone to Jessie.

"Hi, Dad."

"Hello, honey," Merle said. "Sounds like you had quite a day."

"It was fun, but tiring. What is it about swimming that makes you feel so drained?" she asked, sinking into a chair.

Merle laughed. "I don't know, but I know what you mean."

"By the way," Jessie said. "I'm mad at you."

"Mad? Why?"

"Why didn't you call when you got in Saturday evening and let me know you made it all right?"

Merle didn't want to tell her he hadn't left until Sunday morning because of the visit he and Vera had made to Dan. Urging forth an apologetic chuckle, he said, "I'm sorry, honey. I guess I'm just not used to letting people know what I'm doing."

"I'll buy that," she replied with understanding, "but I'd still like to have known."

"I did try to call all day today."

"Okay, okay, you're forgiven!"

Merle laughed. "I wanted to let you know that I miss you and Cissy already."

"Well, why don't you pack up and move over here?" she suggested breezily.

He sighed. "I thought about it, but unfortunately, I can't just up and leave the company."

"I know," she told him solemnly. "But we can visit more often."

"Yes. And we will."

"Promise?"

"Promise."

"I'm holding you to it."

"I expect you to," Merle told her with a laugh. "Jessie, there's something else I wanted to talk to you about."

Jessie didn't miss the new, more serious note in his voice. "Sure. What is it?"

"Do you remember what you said about your dream?"

"Yes. Why?"

"Well, how would you like for it to come true?"

"That would be great," she said, giggling girlishly. "What did you do? Find Aladdin's lamp?"

She could hear the responsive humor in Merle's voice as he replied, "No. But I do know a good lawyer."

"I'm sorry, Dad, but I don't get it."

"Oh, yes, you do," he said cryptically.

"Whoa! Wait! I'm lost," she cried, flinging up her hand in a gesture he couldn't see. "I really *don't* get it."

"Yes, you do. I'm giving it to you."

Jessie put her palm to her forehead, smiling at the confusing conversation. "I feel like Abbott and Costello doing the 'Who's On First' routine," she teased. "Do you mind clarifying *it*?"

"Not at all," he teased back in a magnanimous voice. "I went to my lawyers this morning and made arrangements to have all my thoroughbred holdings transferred to you immediately."

Jessie wasn't certain she'd heard right. Was it possible that he was going to let her have a couple of horses? She knew from the form that he had some superb horses running well back east. "That's great, Dad, but why?"

"You're my only child, aren't you?"

Growing happiness made her quip cockily, "I dunno. Am I?"

"Cheeky kid!" Merle snorted. "Will you stop being so cute and listen to me?"

"Yes, sir," Jessie acquiesced, a smile playing at her lips.

"I came to look you up for a special reason, Jessie. I wanted to see you, get to know you and if you were half the woman I expected you to be, I was planning on leaving all my thoroughbred holdings to you when I die."

"Die!" Pictures of Merle wearing a suit that hung on him, Merle pale and tired, Merle resting so often flitted darkly through her mind. She gripped the phone with white-knuckled fingers. "Dad, you're okay, aren't you?"

"Of course I'm all right," he told her with a hearty laugh.

"Then what's all this about leaving things to me when you die?"

"There's just no getting around it, honey. I'm not getting any younger."

"I don't want to hear this," Jessie said, meaning every word.

Realizing they were getting into dangerous territory, Merle sidestepped it with another attempt at humor. "You don't have to. I changed my will. Instead of waiting until I die to give you the things I want you to have, I'm making arrangements for you to have them in your possession immediately, just like I told you earlier."

Tears swam in Jessie's eyes. "Dad, that's great! I can sure use a couple of good horses."

"A couple? Jessie, I have almost twenty head of horses in training across the country."

"Twenty head!" Jessie squealed.

"Yes. And they aren't dinks, either. I've picked and culled, and most of them are paying their way. Several are making really big money."

Paying their way. Big money. An owner's dream. A trainer's dream. Her dream. The tears spilled over her lashes and slid down her cheeks. "I don't know what to say," she whispered.

"How about 'Thank you, Dad'?"

Jessie smiled in spite of her tears. "Thank you, Dad."

"You're very welcome."

"Are you sure you really want to do this?" she asked.

"Positive."

"I'll try to do a good job for you, make you some money."

"Jessie, you don't understand. They won't be making me money. As of this morning, they're yours. They'll be making *you* money."

Hers! They were hers! The kind of horses she'd dreamed of. The kind of...

"I'll be mailing you the key to the house," Merle said, interrupting her thoughts.

"House?" she said with a sniff. "What house?"

"The house on the farm."

Her eyes, shining with tears, widened in surprise. "Farm?"

"Yes, farm. I told you I was giving you all my thoroughbred holdings. And that includes a farm in South Louisiana, near Carencro."

"How big a farm?" she asked, overwhelmed by his generosity.

"You know Honey Hill Farm?" he asked.

"Yes," she said with a nod.

"That's it. I'd say it's somewhere in the neighborhood of two hundred acres. It's pipe fenced, has a stallion barn and a training barn and track and comes equipped with three stallions and a couple dozen brood mares and their foals."

"Two hundred acres!" Jessie breathed. "I...I can't believe this."

"Believe it." Merle chuckled.

"But, why?"

"Because I love you and I want to do something for you." Jessie didn't miss the hint of pain that had crept into his voice. "I know giving you things can't begin to make up for all the lost years, but..."

"Dad..."

"I wanted to do something to show you how sorry I am. How much I love you."

"You don't have to do this. I know how much you love me."

"Maybe so. But you haven't had things easy. If your mother hadn't been so stubborn I could have made things better for you both all these years." He sighed heavily. "But that's all water under the bridge now. I can't change the past. The important thing is that I can maybe help change your future. Take them, Jessie," he begged in a gruff voice. "They don't mean anything to me anymore."

"All right. I will." She sniffed again and tried to control the trembling of her lips. "I'll make you proud of me, Dad, I promise."

"I'm already proud of you, Jessie girl. I already am," he said.

They hung up soon after that and Jessie leaped up and grabbed Cissy, whirling her around the living room while they both laughed and Cissy squealed in pleasure, even though she didn't really know what was going on.

Bodie. Jessie twirled to a halt. He was coming over in a little while. She should call and tell him to hurry so she could share her good news...

Before she could get to the phone, someone knocked at the door and, still wearing a silly, satisfied grin, Jessie hurried to open it. Maybe Bodie was earlier than he was supposed to be.

But it was Vera instead of Bodie. When she saw the grin that threatened to split Jessie's face, she asked dryly, "What happened? Did you win the Pick Six?"

"Better," Jessie said with a laugh.

"Better?"

"Grandpa called!" Cissy said, taking Vera's hand and shaking it with a contagious excitement.

Vera's features sharpened in concern. "Merle called? Is everything all right?"

"Everything's great, Mother!" Jessie said, launching into an account of her conversation with her father.

"You're a very lucky girl."

"You'll help me, won't you?" Jessie asked.

"Help you? What do you mean?"

"I mean you've traveled around all your life. Surely you're ready to settle in one spot. I'd like you to run the farm for me."

"Run the farm for you?" Vera asked, a frown slashing two lines between her brows. "What are you going to be doing?"

"I'll be training the other horses."

"Let me think about it," Vera said, stalling. "Have you told Bodie yet?"

"No, I haven't had time," Jessie told her. "I was about to call when you came."

"This is definitely a time for celebration! Why don't I take Cissy home with me to spend the night, and you take Bodie out on the town!"

"Out on the town! I'm broke! I just had work done on my car," Jessie said.

"No problem!" Vera told her, rummaging around in her purse and waving her American Express card grandly.

Jessie took it with a laugh, knowing that no amount of celebrating could make her any happier than she was at that very moment. Everything she'd ever wanted was within her reach at last. Like Vera said, she was a very lucky girl.

Chapter Eleven

When he arrived an hour later, Jessie took Bodie to Jimmy's Lakeside Restaurant on Lake Bistineau. Built of rough cedar on tall piers at the water's edge, the restaurant, which served everything from steak and seafood to Chinese fare, looked out over a bay of houseboats, one of them the familiar turquoise and black Lattimer boat.

The place was a favorite of Jessie's because of its down-to-earth simplicity and excellent food and service. Now, sitting near the windows that overlooked the gently eddying water, she sipped at her wine cooler and tried to stifle the smile that kept struggling to surface.

Bodie leaned back in his chair, laced his fingers together on the top of the table and watched her. No doubt about it, something was going on. Jessie was about to pop out of her skin with excitement, and the fact that he wouldn't give in and ask her what was going on only added to the game she was intent on playing when she'd insisted that she treat him to dinner.

She looked gorgeous. The aura of anticipation surrounding her lent a glitter of gold to her brown eyes and a blush of pink to her cheeks. She had gone all out for the occasion—whatever it was—and dressed in soft sleek slacks and a long silk shirt of jade green that fell away from the slope of her breasts in an enticing manner. Her hair was done in a French braid that hugged the contour of her head and was the perfect foil for the huge gold hoops dangling from her ears. The hollows in her cheeks and the enchanting shadows around her eyes were enhanced by the skillful application of her makeup. Her lips, shining with a dewy gloss, were kissably, deliciously red; her lashes looked at least an inch long. Bodie damned their platonic agreement, which whispered to him that the desire stirring to life inside him was futile.

"Aren't you ever going to ask?" she said at last.

His heavy black brows lifted in question and his mustache hiked up at the corners in a slow smile. "Ask what?" he rumbled huskily.

Jessie saw the twinkle in his eyes. Her own eyes narrowed in mock anger at his deliberate ploy to bait her with his seeming obtuseness. "Beast!" she hissed through straight white teeth.

Bodie smothered another smile and raised his glass of beer in a mocking salute. "If you say so."

"You can't fool me. You're dying to know what's going on."

He downed a mouthful of the brew and said, "Yeah, I am. But I can tell by that smug little smile of yours that you aren't going to tell me until you're good and ready."

Jessie's head canted to the side and she regarded him through her lashes. "I guess I've kept you in the dark long enough," she said. "Merle called this evening."

"Did he make it back all right?"

"Yes." She traced the rim of her glass with one coral-tipped finger. "He gave me some very good news."

"I can tell that. What was it?"

Renewed excitement transfixed her features. "He's giving me all his thoroughbred holdings."

"That's great, sweetheart!" Bodie said, his initial reaction one of happiness. She deserved something good to happen...especially now, with Dan's threat hanging over her head.

"You won't believe what all it entails!"

Bodie considered that statement carefully. Merle Harper. Owner of one of the biggest sugar factories in Florida. Money. Power. Fairly visible within the world of thoroughbred horse racing. "All it entails" could be quite extensive...horses, land... The pleasure her announcement had evoked drained from him like water through a sieve and was replaced with a nebulous fear. His cheeks felt cast in a cement smile. "What does it entail?"

Jessie rattled off the figures Merle had recounted; Bodie felt his own fears taking shape. "So what do you think?" she asked in breathless waiting.

I think we're in trouble, sweetheart. Dear God, I hope not, but I'm really afraid we are. Had Jessie taken him up on his love because she didn't think her other goal was within reach? He pushed aside the nagging doubts and, reaching for her hand, gave it a gentle squeeze. "I think it's fantastic, Jessie," he lied. "And you sure as hell deserve it."

That part wasn't a lie. It was the dream she'd chased for over six years, handed to her on life's silver platter. Everything she'd wanted was finally within her grasp. He loved her better than life itself, and this moment of her triumph should have been sweet for them both. But the news wasn't sweet. It was a bitter pill to swallow, laced as it was with the fear growing within him that he had only been second choice.

"Bodie?" she asked, tugging on his hand to get his attention. "Is something the matter? You aren't listening."

His mind came back from its grave musings and his eyes found hers. "Sure I was," he replied. "Two hundred acres is a nice little spread."

"Little!"

"You know what I mean," he said, conjuring up another fraudulent smile.

Jessie smiled back, and he thought again how beautiful she looked. The waitress arrived with their food and Bodie gave Jessie's hand a final squeeze. "I'm proud of you, sweetheart. I hope you make a million bucks three times over."

"I just might," she said, meeting his gaze and wondering where the light in his sparkling green eyes had gone. He said all the right words, and there was a hint of a smile on his face, but a tiny voice inside her whispered that something wasn't quite right.

After they finished their dinner, Jessie, who decided that the momentary lapse in her happiness was founded on nothing more than the fact that she wasn't used to such good fortune and was therefore afraid it would be snatched away, asked Bodie to take her on a short cruise on the houseboat.

Outside, Jessie threw her head back, laughing as the sharpening wind whipped her exhilaration into a wild frenzy. Happiness had gone to her head like strong drink, he thought as they walked hand in hand down the uneven boards of the pier where the boats were anchored in a row. She was nothing at all like the serious Jessie he knew so well.

A rising wind sent the heavy, wind-tossed clouds that were moving up from the gulf scudding across the sky. Far away, a rain crow called and thunder rumbled an ominous warning. Bodie helped Jessie jump to the deck and untied the boat from its mooring, unable to shake the feeling that nature was getting in tune with his feelings and fears.

He seated himself on a tall stool behind the steering wheel and turned the key. As usual, the engine cranked to instant, chugging life and he reversed the boat out of her spot and headed out toward the main channel of the lake, careful, as the sign on a cypress tree warned, to leave no wake in the small, secluded bay. Once out in the large open area of the lake, he throttled the boat to a higher speed, guiding it easily through the evening that was deserting them in face of the approaching storm and the night.

Inside the cabin, Jessie stood at his side, watching the shoreline go by through the screened sliding door, listening to the quiet thrumming of the engines and smelling the evocative scents of summer and faraway rain carried on the wind that blew in through the open door. Life was good, she thought, a dreamy, satisfied smile bowing her lips. She had it all now. Bodie. Merle. Her dream. Cissy. The smile on her face fled at the thought of her daughter. That was the only fly in the ointment. The only blemish on the face of her life. Did she have Cissy?

A chill tripped over her body, leaving behind an uneasy feeling and a rash of goose bumps that had nothing to do with the cool breath of the storm rushing through the doorway and taking the heat from the cabin. In an act as instinctive as drawing her next breath, Jessie slipped beneath Bodie's arm to stand in the vee of his legs and the irregular circle made by his arms.

She wondered if she only imagined that he stiffened when her arms slid around his middle and her hands began to move up and down over the firmness of his back. Surely she must have, because she felt the subtle play of muscles rippling beneath her sensitive palms when he drew her closer with one arm. His heart beat out a regular cadence beneath her cheek. It had been an exhausting day. Her eyes fluttered shut. Peace. Home. She sighed. Bodie...

She didn't know how long she stood in his embrace, hovering in that realm somewhere between sleep and wakefulness. The motor stopped, drawing her unwillingly from her lethargy. She lifted her head and looked to see where they were.

Bodie had brought the boat to a stop in a small cove ringed by trees whose branches danced in the freshening wind. Far across the lake she could see the lights of several houses, but there was no light here except theirs. She looked up at Bodie in question, and his answer was to jerk her to him with a brutal force that took her by surprise. She gasped as he took her mouth in a ravenous kiss, crushing her lips beneath the bruising punishment of his while his hands sculpted her head in a hard grip.

If he expected withdrawal, he was disappointed. Instead of pulling away, Jessie opened her mouth, welcoming the probing thrust of his tongue. Her upper body pressed against him, and he suddenly realized that her small, firm breasts were bare beneath their silk covering.

Exultation sent his spirits soaring, partially eradicating the feeling of doom that had held him in its clutches since she'd told him her news. She was still his. Nothing had changed. His kiss gentled and his hands began to work through her hair, finding and removing the pins that held the braided knot coiled at the base of her neck. Her mouth moved hotly beneath his while he worked to free her hair from its bondage. He sifted his fingers through the silken strands, warm from her body heat and radiating a subtle hint of perfume.

He took his mouth from hers to plant a row of moist kisses along her jawline to her ear. "You smell so good," he whispered, his breath a tickle that sent a frisson of desire scampering down her backbone to settle with throbbing intensity in the very core of her womanhood.

"So do you," she whispered back, drawing in another shallow, shuddering breath and filling her nostrils with a purely masculine scent that had tormented her all evening. It was the aroma of tobacco and men's cologne, with an underlying scent of no-nonsense soap. It was a smell that whispered of pirates and riverboat gamblers and cowboys who wooed and won women with a smile and a sweeping flourish of their hats. Men who gambled at life and played to win.

He reached to flip off the cabin's lights. If only she knew. That was exactly what he was doing. He was playing to win with the only hand fate had dealt him, gambling on the searing and unaccountable desire that bound them irrevocably together. He was gambling that the love they professed and their craving for one another were stronger than the promise of the success she'd always craved, which now dangled before her nose like a carrot on the end of a string.

Vowing that he would make this night so memorable she'd never forget it, he moved his hands beneath the long tails of her shirt, found the elasticized waistband of her slacks and began a slow, measured slide down her body. Bending slightly and sending her recently freed hair over her shoulder in a shining cascade, she stepped from her pumps and peeled the panty hose down her long legs, kicking the small pile out of the way with a bare foot. She straightened and gave her head a toss, flinging the hair out of her eyes and back over her shoulder. Then she looped her arms around his neck and eyed him with a challenging regard.

Bodie picked up her nonverbal gauntlet. His hands moved to the backs of her thighs and drifted upward,

rough calluses against smooth flesh. They slipped up
to cradle the roundness of her derriere, and he realized with a start that her panty hose were the only
covering she'd worn.

His questioning look brought an impish, sexy smile
to her lips. She laughed, a soft sensual sound that
caused a tightening in his loins.

He groaned and shifted closer to the edge of the
stool where he sat, pulling her against him. This wasn't
the same Jessie who'd been afraid to make love the last
time they were together on the boat. This Jessie was
confident, sure of herself. He was glad to see her this
way, but tormented by the fact that it was Merle's gift
that had done this to her. *Why didn't my love do this
for you, Jessie? Why?*

She leaned forward and pressed her lips to his—a
kiss so soft he might have only imagined it.

*Dan and his threats be damned! This is my night,
and I want it... all of it...* was his last conscious
thought before Jessie initiated her seduction.

The bristles of his mustache rasped gently across her
tongue as it traced the curving edge of his lip. Her
hands moved from his neck to the back of his head
just before she reached the first crest that created the
exciting masculine shape of his upper lip. His lips were
soft, she thought in wonder. Incredibly soft, really, for
a man who looked so tough, so hard. She sifted her
fingers through his hair and paused in her exploration to imprint his mouth with a series of easy, moist
kisses that he returned in kind.

Abandoning her exploration of his mouth, she
pulled his head against her breast, just holding him,
trying to decide when she had ever loved him more

than she did at this precise moment. Eyes closed, she listened to the lapping of the wind-churned water against the pontoons, felt the damp heat of his breath against the gentle curve of her breast and tasted the sharp tang of excitement rising within her as his mouth nuzzled at the silk covering her breast and found her nipple with unerring skill.

His teeth closed with exquisite care over the hard button and loosed the sound of her harsh, indrawn breath, a sound that was almost hidden by the sharp staccato of rain that flung itself without warning against the metal roof. Neither noticed the increasing rainfall as the tip of his tongue teased her with rapier-like flicks that soon grew unsatisfactory and necessitated a need for more.

Jessie's hands held him to her, and Bodie's mouth opened, taking the entire peek and caressing it. Each masterful stroke of his tongue raised the level of her need, wetting the fabric of her blouse and priming her with an answering moisture to ease his eventual possession. Aching for that possession, she arched against him, feeling the undeniable proof of his arousal straining the bonds of his already too-tight jeans.

His hands slid up beneath the silken top, cupping her breasts and bringing a sigh of pleasure to her lips. His knuckles grazed the pebble hardness of one nipple. Then his hand drifted down over her ribs, the backs of his fingers dipping briefly into her navel before skimming the flat plane of her stomach and reaching the delta at the juncture of her thighs. He covered the mound of her femininity with the warmth of his palm. Needing to feel the completeness that her possession brought him, he began an exploration of the hidden places of pleasure secluded within the silken folds.

Jessie's head fell back, exposing her neck. She shifted her hips and found the rhythm that matched his questing fingers.

Suddenly and without warning, Bodie reached the end of his tether. Whether it was the fact that he would never have enough of her, or the overwhelming need to stamp her with the mark of his possession, he didn't know. He only knew he couldn't wait any longer.

With a muffled exclamation of impatience, he scooped her up into his arms and carried her to the boat's small bedroom. With Jessie's help, his clothes were stripped from him in record time, and he joined her on the bed just as a boom of thunder and a roiling wave pitched the boat and sent it into a bucking roll.

His face was a study in desperation. Reaching up, she framed his cheeks with her palms and stroked the deep grooves scoring his cheeks in an effort to ease the feelings inside him. She knew about desperation. It was a demon that rode her as well. Responding to her gentle touch, he turned his head and pressed a kiss to her palm before positioning himself above her pliant body and with a single breathtaking thrust plunged them both into a maelstrom of pleasure.

There was nothing gentle about their possession of one another. Bodie took her with a purpose and force that matched the storm lashing the boat. Moans of pleasure fought to be heard over the wailing of the wind. Seductive movements of hips rolled in perfect synchronization with the motion of the wave-rocked boat. Kisses seared bare flesh like the lightning outside seared the surrounding countryside.

Bodie loved her with a strength that might have been brutal if Jessie hadn't given back thrust for heady thrust, and if she hadn't been driven by the same need that tormented him: the need to reaffirm that they belonged to one another.

Thunder rolled sullenly in the distance as the storm, brief but wicked, blew over the lake, moving north, toward Arkansas. Side by side, mouth to mouth, hearts beating together as one, Bodie spoke against her lips. "I love you, Jessie."

"I love you, too," she whispered with a sigh, sliding the smoothness of her leg between the hair-crisped length of his.

If ever there was a time to ask, it was now, while they were both sated with lovemaking, while their bodies were still one and his doubts were buried beneath the heavy weight of pleasure surrounding them. He moved back from her a bit, his eyes drifted open and his gaze moved with lazy satisfaction over her face. "Marry me."

He meant for it to sound forceful, but instead he thought he heard a thread of pleading in the words.

Jessie's eyes flew open. The old fear—the fear she thought she'd conquered—that she would become nothing but an extension of him, reared its head. "Marry you?"

"Yes." He took her hands and pressed a kiss to each palm. "I'm getting older every minute, Jessie." His laughter held a hint of wry amusement. "Just look at me."

"You're beautiful," she told him truthfully. Her fear quieted; Bodie wasn't a threat to her self-image. That was certain. She was her own worst enemy. "And you're not getting old."

"I'll be forty in December, sweetheart, and I want a baby while I'm still young enough to enjoy one. I love Cissy to death, but I want my own child. Our child."

Jessie was still a moment, staring at a point across the bedroom. A baby. Bodie's baby. It was a wonderful thought, a dream she'd longed for, but given up on; still . . .

"Honey Hill is a fantastic place," he told her, trying his best to hide his disappointment that she wasn't showing more enthusiasm over his proposal. "It would be a great place to raise babies and horses."

She nodded with slow consideration as the picture of a dark-haired, green-eyed baby boy took root in her mind. But babies tied you down, and . . .

"Besides," he said, urging a teasing tone he was light years from feeling to his voice, "if you marry me, all your problems with Dan would be solved."

Her gaze moved back to his face. "What do you mean?"

He snapped his fingers in front of her nose. "C'mon, sweetheart, wake up. If we got married, Dan wouldn't have a leg to stand on."

Her problem with Dan would be over. That alone should make her ecstatic, but . . .

Jessie drew her hands free and moved away from him. She felt cold and empty inside without the strength and heat of him inside her. She pushed the scary feeling away and levered herself into a sitting position. A frown wrinkled her forehead as she drew the sheet up to cover her chilling body.

Bodie had the strangest feeling an invisible wall had been subtly erected between them when she drew the sheet up to cover her nakedness. "Jessie? What's the matter?"

She glanced at him out of the corner of her eye before she seemed to become inordinately interested in her fingers, which were busy pleating the floral sheets. "I'm just a little surprised, that's all."

He reached out and placed one finger beneath her chin, lifting her face upward until their eyes met. "Surprised?" he asked in an incredulous tone. "Where did you think all this was going anyway? Did you think all I wanted from you was a roll in the hay every now and then?"

"No. Of course not."

His hand dropped to her sheet-covered hip and began a soft stroking. "Then what is it?"

Candor resided in her brown eyes as she said, "There's been so much going on these last few weeks—you coming back into my life, Merle, the thing with Dan. I guess I haven't been thinking beyond the moment."

"Well, think about it now," he suggested, trying to tell himself he didn't actually hear the clashing notes of steel and fear in his voice.

"You want us to live at the farm?" she asked.

"Yes." He smiled in wry amusement. "I'm not as wealthy as you are now, but I think I can contribute my fair share to a breeding facility and our marriage."

"What about the racing stock?"

"Why can't you start their training on the farm, and then we can turn them over to my brothers?"

Jessie's eyes shifted from his. She fought the frustration building within her. Why hadn't she foreseen this? Why had she assumed that life was suddenly going to be rosy? "You don't want me training, then?"

The cheer in Bodie's voice sounded forced, strained. "It's not the training I object to, but, hell, Jess, it's kinda hard to travel a racing circuit with a couple of kids in tow. You would need to be at home with them."

Jessie wriggled into a better position.

Bodie read the signs of her inner struggle. They only increased his own unease. *Get it over with! Say it, Jessie.*

But in the end, he said it for her.

"It isn't enough, is it?"

The dull tone of his voice, coupled with the statement, rendered her silent momentarily. Still, she thought, she owed him an explanation of how she felt, and there was no reason their marriage couldn't work if she kept on training.

"This is what I've waited for," she hedged. "It's the opportunity I've always wanted. If your brothers are listed as trainers, no one will know that I had anything to do with it. I *need* that recognition, Bodie. I've needed it for a very long time. I'm not certain I can settle for half a dream."

The breath he'd been holding soughed from him in a deep sigh. His eyes probed hers with an intensity that made her want to look away. But she didn't.

"It's my big chance. My only chance," she told him, desperate to make him understand. "I never expected to have anything like this dropped into my lap. I have to make use of it, don't I?"

He sighed again, the thick, dark thatch of his lashes dropping to shut out the sight of her face and the earnest entreaty in her eyes. The hand resting on her upper leg skimmed the length of her thigh, the gentle curve of her hip and the narrow expanse of her waist. Up and down. And up again. Almost as if he were memorizing her through touch, almost as if he were afraid that if he stopped touching her she would disappear... He nodded finally, a nod that underscored his statement. "Yes, Jessie, I guess you probably do."

It was what she wanted to hear, but she felt as if she had just lost something very precious to her. She leaned down to kiss him, and Bodie allowed their lips to touch briefly.

He opened his eyes and met the brown velvet of her gaze at last. "Get dressed, sweetheart," he urged softly, brushing his lips across hers again and turning to get up himself. She reached out and placed her hand on his biceps in an effort to hold him.

Bodie looked from her hand—the capable, clever hand that could soothe a nervous horse or bring a man to exquisite ecstasy—up to her face, which held a montage of conflicting emotions.

"You do understand, don't you?" she asked.

Was that the threat of tears he heard in her voice? Were those tears glittering in her eyes, or a mirage created by the bedside lamp? Or were they wishful thinking? His whole world was going to hell in a hand basket for the second time in his life and all he could do was sit back and watch it happen. Bodie swallowed his own strangling emotion and knew that this time, when it was over, he would need to keep states instead of shedrows between him and Jessie. And he would spend the rest of his life following that gray ribbon of highway from coast to coast.

In the end it was the male pride that Jessie despised and the need to survive emotionally that twisted his sexily shaped mouth into something that passed as a smile and made his voice cool and remote. "You bet I understand."

Desperation sharpened Jessie's tone. "You said you wouldn't mind if I kept working with the horses."

"And I meant it."

You haven't said it, but you want me to stay at home and be a wife and mother...just like Dan. It was more than disappointing to think that Bodie expected the same thing of her Dan had. It was downright hurtful, but there was one major difference. She didn't think she loved Bodie; she knew she did. And she wasn't ready to give up on him—not yet, anyway. She needed him in too many ways. "We could make it work if I keep training."

"Could we?" he retaliated, mockery surfacing in the sea-green depths of his eyes.

"Of course we can!" she said, feeling, as he had all evening, that things were going awry with an astounding, frightening speed.

"It's easy to be noble and give up something you don't have and don't think you can ever get, Jessie. But when that something is in your hand, it isn't so easy, is it?"

"What are you saying?" she asked, afraid to acknowledge the beginning twinges of despair overshadowing over her happiness.

"I'm saying that it was easy for you to say that Cissy and I were enough to make you happy as long as you thought your dream to become a big-time trainer was out of reach."

Jessie couldn't believe she was hearing the accusation in his voice. She couldn't believe he would think that of her. "How can you say that? I love you both. Surely you believe that."

He was silent, staring at her with eyes that were bleak and devil-ridden, eyes that mirrored the hell raging inside him.

He *didn't* believe it. Jessie's heart shriveled in her breast. The nameless fear sprouting in the dark corner of her heart sprang to full size. She watched as he pulled from her hold and swung his legs over the edge of the bed. Reaching for his jeans, he asked, "So what are you going to do about Cissy?"

"What about her?"

He shoved one leg into the sheath of denim. Without looking at her, he reminded, "The custody suit."

"I thought we could see if Merle would help us."

Bodie knew that "we" and "us" included him, but he thought that the likelihood of them ever becoming "we" and "us" had slipped from his grasp some time during the last few minutes...or earlier. Perhaps when Merle had called.

"And if he does help, and you get her for good, what are you going to do? She'll start kindergarten this fall. Who will take care of her while you gallivant all over the country chasing your dream?"

"Mother will be there," Jessie offered with well thought out logic. "She'll be running the farm. Besides, I thought you—"

"Me!" His eyes drilled into hers with frightening intensity. "I work, too, Jess. Or have you forgotten that? I'll be gone a lot. I sure don't plan on being a kept man, and Vera sure as hell doesn't need a child full-time. If you're going to leave her, why don't you let Dan and Francine have her? She needs two parents. That's something you, especially, should be able to relate to."

Jessie looked as if he'd slapped her. Her face was pale as she cried, "Bodie! She's my daughter! How can you even ask that?"

She heard something akin to contempt as he said, "That's right. She's your daughter. I can't believe that you'd go off and leave her after being so afraid that Dan and Francine might get her. She's already had a lot of upheaval in her life. She doesn't need to be abandoned for months on end. You need to be there for her."

"I won't be abandoning her, and I will be there for her."

"From across the country? Via telephone?" he taunted, pinning her with a disgusted look while he jerked on his socks. "That won't cut it, Jess. And this whole thing is a tad selfish, don't you think? Personally, I'm getting a little sick of your selfishness. All you've ever thought of is how you feel... what Jessie wants."

Jessie cringed from his anger. What had happened to the tender lover who'd taken her to glorious heights only moments before? What had happened to the Bodie who was so understanding?

"Why are you doing this to me...to us?" she asked. Her eyes begged for understanding; she got more anger.

He pulled on his shirt and began to button it. "Damn it, Jess! I'm trying to make you see what you're doing to Cissy and me. And yourself."

She might as well not have heard him. She sat up in the bed, pleading with anguished eyes. "Don't do this, Bodie. Please. You know this is my chance to make something of myself. My only chance."

Bodie began to laugh softly. He stood, tucked his shirt into his jeans and zipped them. "You still don't see, do you?"

She was losing him...again. Her heart began to crack inside the constricted cavity of her chest and she wondered why he was being so obstinate when she knew they could work things out, even though to be true to herself there was nothing she could do but exactly what she was doing. "See what?" she cried in complete despair.

Relenting of his fury for at least the moment, Bodie sat down on the edge of the bed and reached out to grasp a handful of her ash-blond hair. His eyes were tender but fringed with a bleakness he couldn't disguise. His voice was a low rumble of pain and regret as he murmured, "You honestly don't know, do you?"

She didn't answer, but only looked at him with pain-shadowed eyes. He smoothed her hair back from her face.

"You're a gutsy lady who had made every man on this racing circuit stand up and take notice. You give them all a run for their money. You know why they don't accept you? They're scared of you, lady. You're a threat to everything they've been brought up to believe about the sacred male sex. You've made them all aware of a woman who's carved out a place for herself—no matter how small a place that may be—in what is still considered a man's world. That's something to be proud of. And that makes you somebody."

Was he right? "Bodie..."

"No. You listen! You're Jessica Lorene Harper. You're beautiful. Smart. There isn't another person like you on the face of this earth. You're Merle and Vera Harper's daughter. They don't have another like you. Never will. Never could. You're Cissy's mother. And a damn good one at that, no matter what Dan tries to prove. And that's the most important job you'll ever have, Jessie. Making Cissy a loving, caring, responsible person—a person secure in who and what she is."

Jessie swallowed back her tears.

"You know how you feel because you were deprived of one parent. Don't make the same mistake with Cissy. Don't deprive her of both her parents. She doesn't need to grow up with your insecurities, just like you don't need to become a successful trainer to prove your worth."

An embarrassed smile curved his mouth. "End of sermon." His hand made one final, lingering sweep of her hair before dropping to the sheet. He stood up, the smile gone. "Get dressed, Jess. I'll take you home."

She watched as he turned and left the boat's bedroom. Then, with a heavy heart and burning eyes, she began to dress.

The ride back to the landing was silent. Bodie mourned the demise of his hopes; Jessie vacillated between fear and despair that she was losing Bodie and a fighting determination that she could do it all...have it all.

Lights on several of the houseboats greeted their arrival, and the sounds of loud voices and a jukebox at the bar situated next to the restaurant wafted through the night air. While Bodie tied the boat, Jessie took his proffered keys and started through the damp night air toward the truck.

They didn't speak during the ride to her trailer. The Bronco's headlights slashed through the night like the memory of their argument slashed at her heart. It wasn't until he pulled into her driveway and shoved the gearshift into park that he turned to her. The moonlight played across his features, glinting off the silver in his hair.

Jessie waited breathlessly. *Tell me it will be all right. Please, tell me it will be all right.* And his first words made her believe it was going to be.

"I love you, Jessie."

Her spirits lifted.

"You've got to be somebody special if I couldn't find anyone else to ease this ache inside me all those years we were apart. And I understand your dreams and how important they are to you," he continued.

Her heart grew lighter. It was going to be all right. He did understand.

"But you have to understand, sweetheart, that I have a dream, too."

Jessie's soaring heart plummeted to the pit of her stomach.

"I'm not getting any younger, Jessie. I think you ought to think things through so you don't make a decision you'll regret."

"Is that an ultimatum, Bodie?" Jessie quipped, seeking refuge in sarcasm. If she hadn't she would have broken down completely.

He shook his head. "No. No ultimatums. What I'm trying to make you see is that we can compromise. I'm not asking you to give up horses or training. All I want is for you to be with us, to work with the horses in a different capacity."

Her brief flash of defiance died a swift and merciful death beneath the weight of his logic.

Taking her chin in his hand, he leaned forward and pressed a dispassionate kiss to her lips. His thumb brushed lightly over her bottom lip. "It's late. You'd better get on inside."

Jessie wanted to hold him to her, wanted to cry, to beg, to plead with him to understand. But she wasn't certain she understood herself. "I love you, Bodie, but I—" she began.

Bodie's fingers moved from her chin up to silence her. "I know."

He didn't want to hear the buts. He already knew them. With their eyes meshed, he leaned across her and opened the door. Neither knew how long they sat there, waiting for the other to make a move. Finally, when Jessie realized she could find no hope, *nothing* in his eyes, she stepped from the truck.

"Call me before you go to work in the morning," he told her, reaching to close the door. "I'll be at my brother's."

She nodded. The door slammed shut. He wasn't pressuring her. He was giving her space to think, time to come to a decision that would be right for them all. Jessie watched him reverse out of the driveway with screeching tires. She watched the Bronco's taillights as the vehicle barreled down the street, glowing red reflected in the puddles of water standing on the road. She watched until they disappeared around the corner. A chill draft of air washed over her and she shivered, wondering why she suddenly felt so cold.

Chapter Twelve

It's the most important job you'll ever have. You don't have to prove you are someone.

The words Bodie had spoken spun through Jessie's disoriented dreams like a 78-rpm record jumping from one monotonous groove to the other.

She would never have thought she could fall asleep after everything that had happened, but at 2:43 a.m. the emotions of the day had pulled her into a world of total exhaustion that robbed her of rest by tormenting her with a montage of ever-changing, frightening dreams.

She was swimming in an ocean dotted with cypress trees, trying to save Cissy from a shark who had a toothy all-American smile. Fear sent her legs scissoring in comical fashion through the water. Just as she reached Cissy, the shark became Francine, who held up the fish Cissy had caught the day she'd fished with Bodie and said, "Sometimes you have to ask for help."

You're a damn good mother, no matter what Dan says.

The water and Francine were gone. She heard Bodie's voice, but it was Dan standing before her, dressed in judgmental robes of black, his wrist handcuffed to Cissy's. Jessie was separated from Cissy forever by the bars of a jail cell that was lined with row after row of winning race pictures.

When she fell onto the cell's cot and began to cry, the dream cell changed into a hospital delivery room. She was cold, so cold, and she hurt so badly. It wasn't her abdomen that hurt, cramped with the pains of labor, but her heart, which pounded heavily, noisily in the white brightness of the silent room while a man with Dan's eyes and wearing a surgeon's mask leaned over her and said, "I'm sorry. We couldn't save your marriage...and it was all your fault."

What about my baby! She tried to ask, but couldn't speak. The doctor, who now had Bodie's eyes, must have known what she wanted because he spoke with Bodie's voice and said, "Baby? What baby? You didn't want my baby. You said you'd rather have this!" And he held up a huge trophy with a horse on top wrapped in a flannel blanket.

No! The scream ripped from her throat in protest, a sound that transposed itself from the realm of dreams to reality, bringing Jessie to wakefulness with a vengeance. She sat up so quickly her head swam.

Panic-stricken, gasping for breath, she stared around the room, the sound of her scream still echoing in her ears. Swallowing the fear in her throat, she raked her hair away from her face with hands that shook, then stared down at them in disbelief. They were wet with perspiration, the same perspiration that drenched the T-shirt she'd changed into when Bodie brought her home.

She rose and went to the bathroom to splash cold water on her face in an effort to cool her heated flesh and wash away the residue of sleep clinging to her. The dreams, though fragmented and crazy, had held two underlying themes: Cissy and Bodie, and her fear of losing them both. Something that, in the clear light of day, she realized she didn't want to do—no matter what it cost her.

It was daylight. She whirled toward the blue and gold bathroom's small window. She'd fallen asleep without setting her alarm and been so tired that she'd slept far beyond her usual time to get up, if the degree of sunshine outside was any indication of the time. Fresh panic sent her flying out the door and down the hall to the living room and the telephone. Bodie was waiting for her to call.

Unable to remember his brother's phone number, she leafed through the directory, her fingers skimming the columns of names until she located the right one. The buttons played a strange, melodic tune as her fingers tapped out the numbers in rapid succession. After several clicks she heard the ringing at the other end of the line. "Hurry... hurry..." she chanted beneath her breath.

Before the second ring was completed, a woman's voice said, "Hello."

"Hello. Is Bodie Lattimer there?"

"I'm sorry, but he left a couple of hours ago."

Jessie blinked. Gone. He was already gone? She glanced at the clock in the kitchen and saw that it was ten to eight. No wonder he was gone. "Okay, thanks."

She rushed into her room to dress, pulling on faded jeans, a tank top and tennis shoes with a speed that might qualify her for a spot in the Guinness record book. Then she was out the door and in her car, speeding toward the track.

The short drive seemed endless, but gave her time to think the dreams through. As she saw it, she could do as she'd done six years ago and give up the happiness she knew she could find with Bodie for a pipe dream. The only difference was that the dream had substance now. It was a goal within her reach at last, but at the cost of her daughter and Bodie. At age thirty, it seemed too high a price to pay for a glory that might be as fleeting as the time it took to run and win a race.

She silently thanked Bodie for forcing her to look at her options. Surprisingly, now that she'd had time to think, the alternative was as exciting as becoming a well-known trainer and held just as much chance for the recognition she needed. Breeding was where it was in Louisiana. A top breeder could make a fortune, and Honey Hill had the potential to become the best breeding facility in the state.

She'd told Bodie that she couldn't settle for half a dream, but what she'd forgotten was that he was part of her dream—maybe the biggest part. If she lost him, all the success in the world wouldn't compensate. And, as he'd told her, she could still train at the farm. If his brothers got the credit as trainers, she would get credit as the owner and breeder. She smiled. How could she lose?

After she talked to Bodie she was going to take things into her own hands about the custody suit. She wasn't going to sit by and let Dan take Cissy away from her. She was going to take Francine's advice in the dream, the same advice Bodie had given Cissy. She was going to ask for help. She was going to go to Dan—she might even take Bodie with her—and talk to him face to face. If necessary, she would ask Francine to speak to Dan. Francine believed Jessie was a good mother. Why couldn't she tell Dan how she felt?

With the choice firmly made, Jessie felt a lightness of heart that had been absent for several days. It was amazing what direction could do for your state of mind.

Pulling into the parking space behind the track, she almost ran to the barn, hardly aware of the smile and wave bestowed on her by the security guard. Vera was filling the hay bags with alfalfa when Jessie careened around the corner of the barn.

"Big night?" Vera asked with an arch of her brows in an oblique reference to the lateness of Jessie's arrival.

Jessie planted her hands on her slim hips and drew in a deep draft of air. "Yeah," she panted. "But not the way you think. Has Bodie been by?"

"No," Vera said. "I haven't seen him. Why?"

Jessie gave Vera a brief recap of her discussion with him and her indecision of the night before, finishing up with her strange dreams and her decision to try to find what she'd been looking for with Cissy and Bodie.

"I never thought I'd say it," Vera said when Jessie finished, "but I think you're making the right choice. He's crazy about you, Jessie. If he's what you want, don't let those insecurities I helped instill in you keep you from fighting for him."

Though Jessie and Vera had wiped the slate clean between them, Jessie couldn't help but feel gratitude for the change in her mother's attitude toward life in general and men in particular. She hugged Vera fiercely and whispered a low "thanks."

Vera returned the hug and then, as if the display of emotion made her uncomfortable, she tugged on Jessie's braid and pushed her away. "Go on over to Cary's barn. He might know where Bodie is."

But Cary Lattimer had no idea where his brother was. All he knew was that Bodie had been sitting in the den near the phone when he'd left the house at five that morning. Thanking him, Jessie stopped by several stables she knew Bodie did work for, without any luck. She checked the racing secretary's office, the track kitchen and even the tack shop. No one had seen him that day, or could offer any suggestions as to where he might be.

By the time she'd run through all the places she could think of, it was nearly noon. Vera had finished and gone home, leaving a note on the tack room door that she would pick Cissy up. Heaving a sigh, Jessie retraced her steps back to her Pinto, her steps slow and heavy, dejection and weariness causing her shoulders to slump and her mouth to turn down.

She just didn't get it, she thought, reaching into her pocket for her keys. It was almost as if he'd disappeared from the face of the earth. Or at least from the track. The hand that had the key pointed at the lock froze in mid-action.

Every drop of blood seemed to drain from her body, leaving her feeling light-headed and nauseated. It wasn't possible...

He was sitting, staring at the phone when I left at five.

Call me. She could still see him sitting in the car, looking up at her with—had it been uncertainty and pleading in his moon-shadowed eyes? *Call me.*

Was it possible that when she had fallen asleep and failed to call him before work, he assumed she had made her decision to go on with her life without him? Not only possible, but probable. Bodie must have thought she'd chosen something else over him for the second time. Jessie forced her trembling fingers to unlock the car. Once inside, she started the engine and pulled out of her parking place with a squeal of rubber against blacktop, her stomach roiling sickeningly with the thought that he might have left again, just as he had six years ago.

A quick stop by his brother's house found neither Cary nor his wife at home to question about Bodie's absence. Jessie had no choice but to go home and wait and see if he called. Instead, she stopped by Vera's apartment. Vera was doing cross-stitch while Cissy sat on the floor, immersed in something on the Disney channel.

Jessie burst through the door and headed straight for one of the blue-padded chrome chairs that went with the glass-topped dining table. "I can't find him," she said without preamble.

"What do you mean?"

"I mean, no one at the track has seen him or talked to him. His brother didn't even know where he was."

"Jessie, you don't think . . ."

Jessie met Vera's troubled eyes. She nodded. "Yes, Mother, I do."

"Then I'd advise you to get busy and try to find him."

"Don't you think I want to? But who do I ask?"

"He has another brother, doesn't he? Check with Brian. And if all else fails, give his mother a call."

Jessie gnawed on her bottom lip. "Yeah. I guess I could do that."

"Do that. And when you find out where he is, go after him. I'll take care of Cissy."

Jessie thanked Vera some four hours later as she packed a small suitcase in preparation for her trip. It had taken ages to get through to Bodie's mother, who told her he had gone to Lexington, Kentucky. Like a good mother should, she even knew which motel he was staying at.

Jessie's reaction was one of thankfulness that she'd found him. Keeping him had taken on the same importance as keeping Cissy. She couldn't let him just walk out of her life again.

She was almost finished with her packing when someone knocked at the door. "Not now," she muttered under her breath as she stalked to the living room. "I don't have time for this now."

The door opened with a quick twist of the knob. Jessie's mouth fell open and her eyes widened in disbelief. Standing there, looking as uncertain as she usually felt in their presence, stood Dan and Francine.

"Hello, Jessica," Dan said.

Bits and snatches of her dream flashed onto the screen of Jessie's mind. Dan in the black robes of a judge. Dan with Cissy, separating her from the child. Apprehension coiled loosely in the pit of her stomach. There could only be one reason Dan would come to see her. Cissy. Jessie wondered what new kind of mental torture he had in store for her. She couldn't hide the hesitancy in her voice. "Hello."

Dan's gaze traveled slowly over her stylish khaki slacks and the matching white, black and khaki-striped shirt. "Are we interrupting anything? Were you going out?"

I'm going after Bodie. She wanted to say it, but how could she tell them that? "Nowhere special," she lied, crossing her fingers behind her back as she'd seen Cissy do numerous times. Her gaze moved from Dan to Francine.

Francine knew. Woman's intuition or something, Jessie wasn't sure what, but Francine knew she was going to see Bodie. She watched as Francine's mouth curved into a slight smile. Francine knew, and she didn't care.

"We'd like to talk to you a minute, if you don't mind," Dan told her, pulling her wandering attention back to him. "May we come in?"

"Oh. Sure," she said, stepping aside. Jessie led the way to the living room, never so aware of just how battered her sofa was and just how badly she needed to replace the curtains until Dan stepped inside her house. With his flair for melodrama, would he now tell the judge Cissy lived in a hovel?

She sat down and watched as they seated themselves on the faded floral sofa. "Can I get you something to drink?" she asked in a belated effort to act the gracious hostess.

"No, thank you," Dan said, sounding stilted, as usual.

"We had a late lunch," Francine tacked on. It seemed to Jessie that there was something in the younger woman's eyes that hinted at compassion. She was getting conflicting signals from Francine. What on earth was going on?

Deciding to take the bull by the horns, she looked from Dan to Francine and back again, then blurted, "If you've come here about Cissy—"

"We have," Dan interrupted.

Even though she was choking on her fear, Jessie's voice cut through his. "If it's about the custody suit—"

"Jessie, please," Francine begged in a soothing tone. "Just listen."

Jessie nodded and sat back in her chair, knotting her fingers in her lap.

Dan cleared his throat, the only indication that he wasn't his usual suave and secure self. "Your mother and father came to see me Saturday."

Jessie jerked upright in the chair. "What!"

"Considering everything you'd told me about their past relationship, I was surprised, too," Dan said with a slight shrug. "At first I thought you'd sent them, but your father made it very clear that you knew nothing about it."

"I didn't even know they'd seen one another," Jessie admitted, wondering when and how Merle and Vera had cleared up their past. "What did they want?"

"They wanted to talk to me about the custody suit."

"What!" she cried again. After all her mother's sermons about staying out of other people's business, it seemed impossible that she would act contrarily, but then, Dan wouldn't be there if it weren't the truth.

"They asked me to reconsider." There was a hint of grudging admiration in his half smile. "Your father even threatened me—gently and unobtrusively, of course."

Jessie's head moved from side to side in a negative motion. "I can't believe this."

"It's true," Francine said.

Jessie could hardly doubt Francine's endorsement. "I really didn't know they were planning anything like this."

"I know that."

It must only be her imagination that made it sound as if there were a husky note in his voice.

"I think you ought to know that it's obvious they both love you very much." He cleared his throat. "I know you always worried about that."

Jessie blinked back the stinging moisture gathering beneath her eyelids. They had actually banded together for her. "Yes."

He offered her a strained smile. "Frankly, when they showed up I was as mad as hell." He paused and looked at Francine, who gave him an encouraging nod. Then, meeting Jessie's eyes again, he continued, "But after thinking things over, I have to admit that they're probably right."

"About what?"

"It would be unfair of me to deprive Cissy of your influence. Vera made it very clear how Merle's absence affected you and how her bitterness had influenced your life and decisions."

Jessie knew what it must have cost her mother to spill her innermost feelings—and flaws—to anyone, especially Dan. She swallowed the lump of emotion in her throat.

"After living with you, even for such a short time, I knew what she meant. I've had my own share of bitterness, and I don't want Cissy to wind up that way." Then, as if he knew he'd slighted Jessie in some way, he said, "I mean . . ."

Jessie couldn't help the elation replacing the apprehension in her heart any more than she could help the tears that glittered in her eyes. "I know what you mean, Dan. I don't want that either."

Without either of them being fully aware of it, Francine slipped down the hallway.

"She's really special, Jessie. I'm proud of her. Francine made me see that Cissy is so open and honest and polite and well-adjusted because of you. I certainly haven't done it just by having her on weekends."

"You're good with her," Jessie offered. "And she loves you very much."

Dan's smile could have been classified as sheepish. "Probably because I spoil her. I'm not above a bribe to get results."

Jessie understood. She'd resorted to bribery herself a time or two. "I don't think so."

The uneasy look came back. "Francine also pointed out that we were hardly innocent of what I was accusing you of. She made me realize I'd be a fool to try to take Cissy away from you, and that it would only make her hate me in the long run. And I don't want that."

"Neither do I."

Silence reigned while Dan digested Jessie's comment. He leaned forward, resting his elbows on his knees, his clasped hands dangling between them. "It's Lattimer, isn't it? It always has been."

Shock held Jessie's voice captive.

"You're in love with Bodie Lattimer. And you loved him even while we were married."

Shame sent scarlet color rushing into her face. Confronted with Dan's honesty, could she be less than honest with him? She forced herself to meet his gaze. "Yes."

He nodded in acceptance.

"I never meant it to be that way, Dan," she explained. "I convinced myself that I did love you. It was only recently that I realized that I really hadn't. I think that's why I've felt so guilty about our marriage failing. Deep down, I knew it was all my fault."

"It's never all one person's fault, Jessie," he said, unaware that for the first time since he'd met her he used the shortened version of her name. "I think that some part of me realized you really didn't love me. But I loved you, so I married you anyway, and that means I was as much to blame as you."

Jessie blinked her lashes at a furious speed in a continuing battle to hold the tears at bay. "Thank you for telling me that."

Dan cleared his throat and looked away to hide his own emotion. "I just wanted to come by and let you know that I took action to stop the custody suit yesterday."

She sniffed. "Thank you."

From the corner of her eye, Jessie noticed that Francine had come back into the room. As if it were his cue, Dan rose.

"Are you and Lattimer getting married, then?"

Jessie didn't have the heart to tell him she might have messed up her life a second time. "I hope so."

He nodded.

Francine went to Dan and put her arm around his waist. He circled her shoulders with his arm and dropped a light kiss to her lips. "Come on, Frannie. Let's go home."

Jessie followed them to the door. Before Francine could start down the steps, Jessie put her hand on the younger woman's shoulder. Francine turned, a question in her eyes.

Jessie held out her hand, palm up. "Thank you."

Francine took Jessie's hand and smiled her all-American-mom smile. Jessie thought how wholesome and pretty she looked. Then Francine gave her hand a brief squeeze and turned to follow Dan down the steps.

Jessie leaned against the doorjamb, a sigh of relief and happiness fluttering from her lips as she watched them drive away.

Bodie peered into the shower-steamed mirror and probed the cut on his jaw with a tender touch. The joker must have had on a signet ring of some sort. Reaching for the alcohol, he moistened a cotton ball and dabbed it on the cut, gritting his teeth against the pain. *You play; you pay.* His mother's unforgettable and true words. Would he ever learn?

The day had been one of the longest he'd ever spent. The flight from Shreveport to Lexington seemed endless. When he'd found a room, he'd rented a car and gone straight to the farm where he planned to work and immersed himself in filing and pulling teeth. Even with his late start, he'd done ten head, working long past suppertime in an effort to forget that Jessie hadn't called.

It hadn't worked.

He'd made his decision long ago but, even though it was made, he didn't have to like the way things were going. That he was a fool rankled. But fool or not, he thought on a wave of rebellion, he could have a good time, couldn't he?

His first stop after a shower had been the famous Joe's Bar and Grill.

The food tasted like cardboard. The beer was flat. The woman in his arms on the dance floor felt different than Jessie. And when—after innumerable playings of "You Must Not Be Drinking Enough"—some jake leg down the bar said he wasn't about to listen to it again, it had been all too easy for Bodie to say, "So what are you gonna do about it?"

Giving a grunt of disgust, he pulled back his bottom lip and ran his tongue over the cut inside. He swore roundly and felt somewhat better. Then, rinsing his mouth out with the sample of mouthwash the motel provided, he flicked off the light and crossed to the bed, easing his tired body between the crisp white sheets, too beat to even smoke a final cigarette. He turned off the bedside light and shifted around to get comfortable. His head ached. His back protested the firmness of the mattress. His shoulder joint hurt from the fast and furious grinding he'd done.

You're almost forty. Probably arthritis. Damn you, Jessie.

Exhaustion claimed him; her name was his last conscious thought.

He was dreaming.

Jessie was there, leaning over him, her long blond hair tickling his chest, her bare breasts brushing against him. Her mouth—hot and hungry—plundered his, and her hands...ah, damn, her hands were working the magic only Jessie could work.

"Bodie..." she called. "Bodie... Look at me."

But he was afraid to. He didn't want the dream to end...couldn't bear it. His hands reached to hold her to him before the dream could fade, but instead of ephemeral dream stuff, his hands encountered the warmth of real flesh. He gripped her tighter.

And then Jessie's voice was laughing in his ear. But it was a laughter that sounded threaded with tears. "You're hurting me, you beast. Wake up!"

His eyes flew open at the command, and he knew without a doubt that it wasn't a dream. Jessie was there, her features barely distinguishable in the darkness of the room. He rolled her to her back; his hands moved to her face and his mouth swooped to take hers. Ignoring the small pain of his cut mouth, he kissed her hungrily, needing to prove that she was real.

Jessie kissed him back. She was real. Not a dream. He broke off the kiss and had to ask, even as she pressed her lips to his shoulder. "What are you doing here, Jessie?"

Her voice was husky, throaty-sounding in the darkness. "I fell asleep and didn't wake up until you were already gone. No one knew where you were. No one had seen you. It took me until noon to figure out that you thought I'd chosen racing over you." He heard her sigh. "I knew you'd never come back this time. So I decided to come after you."

Bodie digested her words. "How did you find me?"

"I...called...your...mother," she said, punctuating each word with a kiss on a flat brown nipple. "And," she said, while her hands inched over the hair-whorled plane of his chest, "I bribed the desk clerk for your key."

"You what!"

Jessie reached up and cradled his cheek in her palm. "I bribed the desk clerk. Now will you shut up and kiss me?"

Bodie slid his hair-dusted leg along the smoothness of hers and complied with her request, taking her parted lips with a thoroughness that left them both breathless. "Why?" he murmured against her ear.

"Why what?" she purred, arching her back and rubbing her breasts against his chest.

"Why did you come?" he asked, brushing a strand of hair from her cheek.

Jessie relaxed against the pillows and nuzzled her face in the springy hair of his chest, breathing in the enticing male scent of him. Her hands slid in slow motion down his chest and stomach. "I can raise horses without you, but I can't figure out how to have those babies alone."

Bodie drew in a sharp breath as her hand closed lovingly around him. Only by extreme concentration could he keep his mind on his questions. "What about your dream, Jess? What about being somebody?"

"Later, Lattimer," she urged against his lips as her hand began a slow seduction. "Whatever happened to my man of few words?"

Her words and her touch robbed him of coherent thought. He hesitated only long enough to check her readiness with a softly stroking finger. Finding her more than ready, he grasped both her hands and, pinning them above her head with his, eased into the soft, welcome heat of her. Lowering his head, his mouth found the tautened tip of her breast and began series of nibbling kisses.

"I . . . decided," she began as their hips joined in a slow grinding cadence, "that . . . you were—oh, Bodie, you're driving me crazy—right."

He released one hand to cup a breast, thumbing the moist nipple with exquisite tenderness. She moaned, then said in a rush, "I am somebody. And I can be somebody married to you and . . . Bodie, please—" she sighed "—living at the ranch."

"Please what?" he asked, withdrawing from her almost completely.

"I'm going to kill you later," she promised through clenched teeth, pulling her other hand free. She clasped his bare bottom and pulled him closer so that he filled her once more.

She felt him smile against her lips. Jessie was here. He could afford to relax some. And he could make her pay for tormenting him. "And who is that somebody?"

Thoughts scattered to the four winds by the increased rhythm of his hips, Jessie could hardly remember what she'd been saying. "What?"

"Who have you decided that you'll be?" he asked breathlessly as their dance of love transposed to a faster tempo.

"Jess . . . Jessie Lattimer," she panted. Her hands slid up over his sweat-slickened back. "You know . . . Jessie Lattimer . . . the most successful breeder . . ."

"Of babies or horses?" he interrupted, stopping his movements completely and staring down at her in the darkness.

"Damn you, Bodie..."

His laughter was a low rumble in his chest as he rolled onto his back. Jessie sprawled on top of him. In a position of power at last, she began her own seductive movements. He could hear the cocky lilt in her voice as, instigating each breath-robbing thrust, she said, "I'm Jessie Lattimer, the woman who was woman enough to catch that handsome tooth man— uh, what's his name?—and whip him into husband material."

With lightning quickness Bodie rolled her beneath him once more, all teasing gone as, with one final movement, he hurtled them heedlessly into the hot sea of desire where, at last, all old hurts and doubts were washed away in the purity of their love.

It was good. Right. And somehow, they both knew that this time it was forever.

Later, when the ragged sounds of their breathing had stilled and Jessie was snuggled close to his side, Bodie flipped ashes from the inevitable cigarette and asked, "You wasted your plane fare, you know."

"Wasted! What are you talking about?" she asked, rising up on one elbow and glaring at him. She fumbled for the switch of the bedside lamp, turning it on and flooding the room with soft light. "What do you mean?"

He blew a stream of smoke toward the ceiling and glanced at her out of the corner of his eyes. "I hadn't left for good, Jessie. I was coming back to you. Coming back for you."

"What!"

He twined his fingers through a strand of silky blond hair and wound it around his wrist, drawing her closer. "I told you when I came back here, I meant to have you. Have you forgotten?"

She shook her head. "No, I haven't. But why did you leave?"

He grinned. "I told you over a week ago I had to come here and do some work. It must have slipped your mind."

He was right, she thought with a sinking feeling. He had told her. Embarrassment warred with indignation. Indignation won. "Do you mean that I nearly killed myself getting here, and all for nothing?"

Bodie gave the skein of hair another twist around his wrist, reeling her closer still. There was a decidedly naughty look in his smoky-green eyes as he said, "Well, I wouldn't say it was for nothing."

She stared at the strong masculine face she loved so well, from the bold sweep of his eyebrows to the sensual turn of his mouth beneath the sexy brush of mustache. Reaching out, she traced the crease in one cheek with her fingertip and kissed him softly. Then, with a low, sexy laugh, she snatched the cigarette from his fingers, ground it out and pushed him back onto the pillows with a hard shove.

He didn't like the gleam of mischief in her eyes, but he loved her renewed exploration of him. "What do you think you're doing?" he rasped in a husky voice.

"I think," she told him with a saucy grin, "that since it's become obvious that I messed up, I might as well make the most of a bad situation."

Bodie's laughter was silenced by her warm mouth.

That was his Jessie—sure, confident in herself, and with an ambition and drive to equal his. Jess, with her femininity and her feminine machismo forever warring within her. His Jessie . . . who was all the things that made her so special. Somebody.

His woman.

His love.

His life.

* * * * *

Silhouette Desire

**Available
August 1987**

ONE TOUGH
HOMBRE

Visit with characters introduced
in the acclaimed Desire trilogy
by Joan Hohl!

The *Hombre* is back!
J. B. Barnet—first introduced in *Texas Gold*—
has returned and make no mistake,
J.B. *is* one tough hombre . . . but
Nicole Vanzant finds the gentle,
tender side of the former
Texas Ranger.

Don't miss *One Tough Hombre*—
J.B. and Nicole's story.
And coming soon from Desire is
Falcon's Flight—the story of Flint Falcon
and Leslie Fairfield.

D372-1R

Take 4 Silhouette Romance novels & a surprise gift
FREE

Then preview 6 brand-new Silhouette Romance novels—delivered to your door as soon as they come off the presses! If you decide to keep them, pay just $1.95 each, *(with no shipping, handling or other charges of any kind!)*

Each month, you'll meet lively young heroines and share in their thrilling escapes, trials and triumphs...virile men you'll find as attractive and irresistible as the heroines do...and colorful supporting characters you'll feel you've always known.

As an added bonus, you'll get the Silhouette Books newsletter FREE with every shipment. Every issue is filled with news on upcoming books, interviews with your favorite authors, plus lots more.

Start with 4 Silhouette Romance novels and a surprise gift absolutely FREE. They're yours to keep without obligation. You can always return a shipment and cancel at any time.

Simply fill out and return the coupon today! *(This offer is not available in Canada.)*

For the millions who can't read
Give the Gift of Literacy

One out of five adults in North America
cannot read or write well enough
to fill out a job application
or understand the directions on a bottle of medicine.

You can change all this by joining the fight
against illiteracy.

For more information write to:
Contact, Box 81826, Lincoln, Neb. 68501
In the United States, call toll free: 1-800-228-8813

The only degree you need
is a degree of caring

Sarah

MAURA SEGER

Sarah wanted desperately to escape the clutches of her cruel father.
Philip needed a mother for his son, a mistress for his plantation.
It was a marriage of convenience.
Then it happened. The love they had tried to deny suddenly became a
blissful reality... only to be challenged by life's hardships and brutal
misfortunes.